*Ask Amy Green*

# WEDDING BELLES

*Ask Amy Green*

# WEDDING BELLES

## SARAH WEBB

**CANDLEWICK PRESS**

For Mags Walsh with love and respect.
A true champion of children's books.

Copyright © 2014 by Sarah Webb

First U.S. edition 2014

Library of Congress Catalog Card Number 2013955697
ISBN 978-0-7636-5584-6

14 15 16 17 18 19 BVG 10 9 8 7 6 5 4 3 2 1

Printed in Berryville, VA, U.S.A.

This book was typeset in ITC Giovanni.

Candlewick Press
99 Dover Street
Somerville, Massachusetts 02144

visit us at www.candlewick.com

Dear Reader,

When my sister Emma got married, I was one of her bridesmaids. I wore a turquoise lace dress and, over my shoulders, a little white cardigan with sky-blue flowers embroidered around the neck.

It was a wonderful day, full of joy and laughter. At the reception my two sisters and I (Emma, and Kate, who was also a bridesmaid) sang into champagne bottles along with the ABBA tribute band and then danced till our feet hurt. Weddings are very special events, and it has been so much fun writing about Sylvie and Dave's wedding (Amy's mum and stepdad).

This is the very last book about Amy and all her friends and family. I've loved every minute of writing her story, and I'll treasure Amy and Clover in my heart forever. It's hard to say good-bye to characters that you love, but it's time for me to invent some new characters and to bring *them* alive.

Thank you for reading Amy and Clover's adventures. I hope you have enjoyed reading them as much as I have enjoyed writing them. Thank you to everyone who has written to me over the past few years. I treasure all your letters and e-mails. And look out for my brand-new series in the future.

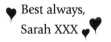

Best always,
Sarah XXX

# ♥ Chapter 1

"What about white doves?" Clover taps her pink gel pen against her teeth. "No, I've got it—butterflies! When Dave and Sylvie are saying their vows, we open a box and *voilà*! Out flutter hundreds of real live butterflies. I saw it in a movie once." Sylvie is my mum, and Dave is her fiancé, soon-to-be husband, if we ever manage to get through our mega-long wedding to-do list.

We're sitting on the small red sofa in my crazy aunt Clover's "office," which is basically a glorified shed at the bottom of her garden. Clover's waving her hands in the air and getting completely carried away with this whole wedding-planning thing. Her large pink notebook is jogging up and down on her knee.

"Clover, that's really cruel," I say. "And where would we get butterflies in April exactly?" Mum and Dave's wedding is on Tuesday, April 30, my fourteenth birthday. Mum asked whether I minded them hijacking my special day, as it was the only day between April and June that the hotel was available, and I said of course not. I mean, what else could I say? At least I'll never forget their wedding anniversary!

"The Internet, of course," Clover says simply, as if it's perfectly normal to buy insects online. "But maybe you're right — it is a bit cruel. And doves might poop on the guests' heads." She pauses, her eyes twinkling. "I wonder if you can train birds to do droppings on particular people's heads. Can you imagine Shelly's face?" She acts out Shelly being pooped on, her eyes popping wide, her mouth pulled into a dramatic wail. "My hair," she squeals, doing a take-off of Shelly's high-pitched, slightly breathy voice perfectly. "Art, I'm being attacked. Save me!" She clutches my arm.

Clover was dead set against Mum inviting Art, my dad, and Shelly, his newish wife, to the wedding, but Mum said that in the "spirit of reconciliation" they both had to be there. Dave just shrugged and said whatever Sylvie wanted was fine by him.

I agreed with Mum. Shelly isn't that bad these days, and my little sis, Gracie, just has to be there.

Shelly has already bought Gracie's outfit, and I can't wait to see her in the adorable teeny-tiny pink-taffeta dress.

"Dad's terrified of birds," I remind Clover. "He'd be straight out of the church screaming as soon as he spotted one."

Clover grins. "Doves it is, then." She's never had much time for Dad. I know he can be a bit self-obsessed sometimes, but he's still my dad. I frown at her.

"Only kidding, Beanie. Settle your tights." She gives a raggedy sigh. "This whole wedding business is tougher than I ever imagined. Who knew there were so many persnickety details to decide on?" She stares down gloomily at her notebook.

"I hear you," I say. "But at least Mum moved the date forward. I know the olds keep saying we can't possibly arrange everything in two months, but are they crazy? Eight weeks is forever."

"True, but after everything that's happened, I want it to be practically perfect in every way. She is my only sis, after all."

Mum and Dave were supposed to be getting married in February, on Valentine's Day, but the date crept nearer and nearer, and Mum still hadn't organized her dress, the food, the invitations, the flowers, the cake. . . . The list was endless. When Clover finally confronted her about it, Mum broke down and admitted that she was freaking out about the wedding plans (not for the first time either) and needed more time to get everything sorted. So Clover offered to help, and she dragged me in as her matrimonial assistant. Now Mum is leaving everything, except choosing her wedding dress, to us. And Clover has cake and pink champagne on the brain. I'm well used to Clover's madcap schemes, though.

As well as attending college to study English and art history, she works as an agony aunt for the *Goss* magazine, answering all the problem letters that readers send in, sometimes solving them in person. We've helped readers with boy dilemmas (Wendy), parental problems (Romie), brother worries (Dominique), and bullying (Alanna). It feels good to be able to help people, and I love spending time with Clover. Mum says that Clover is a force of nature, and I know exactly what she means. Life is never boring with Clover around.

"There's only one thing for it, if we want to get this wedding organized soon," Clover says, sitting up a little. "I was hoping to avoid dragging you into this, but desperate times call for desperate measures. Bean Machine, what are you doing on Saturday?"

I narrow my eyes. What's she up to now?

"It depends," I say carefully.

"Coola boola! Bridal Heaven, here we come."

"Bridal Heaven? What's that?"

"Only the biggest wedding fair in the country. Nuptial nirvana, Beanie, old girl. I have free tickets through a contact at the *Goss*. We'll blitz the place and get the final details of this wedding-schmedding settled once and for all, including Dave's groom's outfit."

I put my head in my hands and groan. "A wedding fair sounds appalling, Clover."

"You could always drag Seth along for the ride."

"Are you bonkers?"

"Frightened he might propose, Love Bean?"

"No! He's fourteen. As if."

"You're right. Seth's too young to be of any use — and he's not Dave's size. But don't worry. I have a dastardly plan, Batman."

"Why does that make me very, very nervous?"

She hoots with laughter. "You love my dastardly plans, Beanie, admit it."

I sigh, then smile. She's right. Even though her plans sometimes hit elephant-size glitches, largely they rock. As I said, life's a lot more interesting with Clover around!

# ♥ Chapter 2

On Wednesday, the sun is shining for a change, so it's warm enough to hang out by the hockey-pitch steps, our usual haunt, during break. I head outside to catch the gang as they come out of class.

My best friend, Mills, is waiting for me by the door, but there's no sign of our boyfriends, Seth and Bailey, yet. They're also best friends, although being boys, they'd never admit it. Mills looks a little glum. Her mouth is turned down, and her eyes are dull and lifeless.

"Hey, Mills, you OK?" I ask her.

She shrugs. "I guess."

It's not at all like Mills to be down. She's usually annoyingly chirpy in school. She's one of those strange people who actually get a kick out of learning random stuff about volcanoes, etc.

"Come on, what's up, Jelly Tot?" I ask.

She shrugs again. "Nothing."

"Tell me right now or I'll tickle it out of you." I poke her in the side. She's ultra-ticklish. You only have to wiggle a finger and say the word "tickle" for her to wince and squirm.

She swats my hand away, scowling. "Stop! I'm not in the mood, Amy."

"Sounds serious. Is it Bailey?"

"No."

"Something at home?"

She shakes her head. I'm not really surprised that nothing's wrong at home. Mills has the calmest, most settled home life of anyone I've ever met, although her sister, Claire, did have some ups and downs recently. She's a ballerina, based in Budapest in Hungary. She had some problems with bullying, but I thought that was all sorted out.

"Is it Claire?" I ask.

"No, Claire's great. Madly in love with Péter and getting all the best solo parts."

"What, then?"

Before Mills can answer, Annabelle Hamilton and her D4 gang pour out of the door in a waft of sickly-sweet perfume and grind to a halt beside us. The D4s are the mean girls in our school, all dyed-blond hair ironed into submission, orange Fake Bake flesh, and super-superior attitudes. And Annabelle's their queen bee.

"Loser alert." Annabelle sniffs the air around Mills. "And, like, what is that horrible stench? Smells like a kid who's wet her knickers. I know — it's fear. Is it because of the Full-up Liberty practice today? Mills, you'd better not wobble and fall off again like you did last week." She gives a nasty sneering laugh right in Mills's face.

Annabelle and Mills are both on the All Saints, the school cheerleading squad. They're supposed to be teammates. There used to be a dozen or so All Saints, but now there are only five — the D4s, Mills, and Nora-May Yang, an American girl who's quite new to the school. Annabelle and her cronies have driven everyone else off the squad. No wonder.

"So much for cheerleader solidarity," I snap at Annabelle, even though I have no idea what a Full-up Liberty is. How dare she be cruel to Mills?

Annabelle wrinkles her nose. "Cheerleader *what*?"

"Look it up, Mensa-meltdown," I say. "It means sticking together."

"Don't mess with me, Green," Annabelle says

with a scowl. "You'll regret it." She flounces off with her groupies tittering behind her before I get the chance to say anything else.

When I turn back to Mills, her face is pale and she looks a bit shaken. "Thanks for sticking up for me, Ames," she says. "But you shouldn't cross Annabelle at the moment. She's been a nightmare since Hugo dumped her last week. Bailey said Hugo gave her the flick to concentrate on his game. Apparently she was a big distraction." Hugo Hoffman is the captain of the school rugby team and Bailey plays left wing. One of the reasons that Mills likes being an All Saint is that she gets to cheer Bailey on when he's playing.

"Being dumped for a rugby ball has got to hurt," I say. "Is this what's worrying you? Annabelle and the abominable All Saints? Why don't you try something different instead? Basketball or cricket. And what on earth is a Full-up Liberty?"

Mills smiles. "It's an American cheerleading stunt that Miss Mallard has adapted for our five-person squad. One girl is backstop. Then three girls — the base — lift another girl up in the air. The girl on top, me, is called the flier. I'm supposed to balance on one leg on their hands, giving a High V."

"A High V?"

She demonstrates: head up, arms stretching into

the air in a *V* shape, fists clenched. She actually looks impressive. Strong and majestic, like the Statue of Liberty.

"I've got really good balance," she continues, "and I know I could nail it if Nina and Sophie kept steady. I wobbled and fell backward last week. It was lucky Miss Mallard caught me on the way down. I could have broken something. Annabelle is backstop, which means she's supposed to stand behind the base and catch me if I fall. She must have taken her eyes off me. And I'm sure she told Nina and Sophie to unbalance the stunt.

"Annabelle's determined to be flier instead of me. She's been picking on me all week. I think she's trying to get me to leave the squad. It's not fair. I'm a much better cheerleader than she is, and I don't want to give up now. I love the actual cheering and I really want to win Nationals. It's all the politics that goes on behind the scenes that I hate."

I smile. "I'm liking this sparky, competitive side, Mills. Who knew?"

"It's not funny. I could have been seriously hurt last week."

"Sorry, you're right. So what are you going to do about it? You can't let Annabelle win, but you can't injure yourself either."

She gives a noisy sigh. "I don't know. Nora-May was the only one who stood up to Annabelle, and she had a bad landing after a Full-up Liberty a few weeks ago and sprained her ankle. She's out of action for a while, so not only do I have to face the D4s alone but we're also a girl down. Miss Mallard is looking for a replacement, but so far she hasn't had any luck. It's terrible timing. We have the trials for the Nationals in a few weeks. All that work for nothing."

I think for a second, then ask, "How hard is a Full-up Liberty?"

"Honestly? Easy-peasy. Especially Nora-May's bit. She just has to push me into the air with Nina and Sophie's help. I reckon even Alex could do it if he was a bit taller." Alex is my two-year-old brother.

Right, I know what I have to do. I take a deep breath and resign myself to my fate. "Mills, I'll replace Nora-May," I say, trying not to sound too gloomy about it. "As a feminist in training, cheerleading is against my religion. However, I'm prepared to make the ultimate sacrifice for my best buddy."

"Seriously? You'd really do that for me?"

"If it stops you breaking your neck and gets you through to Nationals, then, yes. But only until Nora-May's ankle is better. Then I'll happily give her back her slot."

Mills squeals and jumps up and down on the spot. Then she gives me a hug. "You're amazing, Ames, do you know that? You can come to training with me today after school. Miss Mallard will be thrilled I've found a replacement. But you know you'll have to wear a flippy skirt and shake pom-poms, right?"

I bury my head in my hands. "Don't mention the dreaded pom-poms."

"What's this about pom-poms?" Seth asks.

I peel my hands off my face and smile at him. He's walking toward us with Bailey.

"Hi, Seth. How was math?" I ask.

He tips his head to one side. "Why are you trying to change the subject, Amy?"

"Might as well tell them. They'll find out soon enough," Mills says. "Boys, we have rather interesting news. Amy's going to join the All Saints!"

"But you think cheerleading is ridiculous," Seth says. Then he adds quickly, "Sorry, Mills."

Mills smiles. "That's OK. I know she thinks it's silly — which is why she's the most incredible friend in the whole entire universe!"

"I'm joining only to protect Mills from the other pom-pom poodles." I explain to Seth and Bailey what's been happening at cheerleading practice.

Bailey's face darkens. "You should have said

something, Mills," he says, brushing Mills's hair back off her face so that he can see into her eyes.

After giving Mills a hug, Bailey presses his forehead gently against hers. He whispers something in her ear and she smiles. They're locked in their own little world while Seth and I stand beside them awkwardly.

We're not like Mills and Bailey, you see. We don't hold hands walking down the school corridor. We don't have to sit beside each other in shared classes. We don't finish each other's sentences or text each other incessantly. And we don't spend every waking minute with each other.

Bailey often goes back to Mills's house after school for dinner. His dad, Finn Hunter—yes, *that* Finn Hunter, the celebrity chef—is away a lot. His grampa, Mac, is a chef too (but not a celebrity one) and so works evenings. They all live together in Mac's house in Bray. It is a bit of an unusual arrangement, as Finn is not Mac's son, but Bailey seems to love it. Mills goes around there a lot too. Way more than I go to Seth's house.

Don't get me wrong, I love Seth — he's amazing — but I think seeing him all the time would be suffocating. I'm more like Clover than Mills, in that I need my space. Clover adores her rock-star boyfriend,

Brains, but is also happy to fly solo, which is just as well, as he's away touring a lot.

I think giving each other space suits Seth too. He and Polly, his mum, spend a lot of time together. There's only the two of them, and they're pretty close. Polly was really sick last year — she had breast cancer — and for a while Seth was really scared he was going to lose her. She's better now, thank goodness. She's back working too. She's a photographer, and Seth goes on jobs with her sometimes to help with the equipment, which is actually pretty heavy.

Yet, despite all this, as I watch Mills and Bailey, sealed in their own little bubble of love, something claws at the pit of my stomach. They start kissing and my shoulders tense up and my hands screw into balls. *You're jealous, Amy,* a little voice inside my head tells me. *Admit it!*

"Amy?" Seth pulls at my arm. "Why are you staring at Mills and Bailey with that weird look on your face? You've got to be used to their PDAs by now, surely?"

"Sorry, I was miles away. In cheerleading land." I give a theatrical groan.

"Having second thoughts?" he asks. "It's not too late to back down."

"Mills is no match for Annabelle Hamilton, Seth, you know that. The orange-faced one will chew her up and spit her out. Mills needs me, if only to catch her when she falls. And from what Mills was saying about the All Saints' shenanigans, I may mean that literally."

Seth smiles at me. "Which is why you're worth millions of a girl like Hammy Hamilton." It's his nickname for her. He blows his cheeks out like a hamster, making me laugh. "But let's forget about the D4s. They're not worth our time. Hockey-pitch steps? I have some new tunes on my iPod. Want a listen?"

"*Absolument.* Anything to stop me thinking about the pom-poms."

"Hey, lovebirds," Seth says loudly to Mills and Bailey, who are still stuck to each other like limpets. "Stop smooching. We're out of here."

I wait for Seth to take my hand or put his arm around my shoulders, but he doesn't, and we walk toward the steps side by side, bumping shoulders like old friends.

♥ Chapter 3

"What do you think you're doing here, Green?"
Annabelle is standing at the entrance to the girls'
changing rooms, blocking my way in. Her fellow D4
nasties, Sophie Piggott and Nina Pickering, are just
behind her in the doorway. They're already in their
flippy blue All Saints skirts and matching white-and-
blue fitted tops. Mills is in the gym, helping Miss
Mallard put out the mats. The cheerleaders do their
stunts inside to avoid injury. They're not allowed to
do them at the rugby games, in case one of them falls.
The stunts are just for cheerleading competitions.
Which doesn't exactly fill me with confidence.

After Mills told her I wanted to join the squad,
Miss Mallard gave me a very hearty slap on the back
and said, "Well done, Amy. Thank you for stepping

up to the plate for the school. I admire girls with a bit of spirit."

When she'd handed me the uniform, I'd been surprised to find there were no pom-poms. I asked why, but Mills nudged me with her shoulder and laughed. "She's only joking, miss."

That was news to me, and I felt a bit silly, but I said nothing, just pressed my foot against Mills's. Once Miss Mallard had walked away, I turned on Mills. "You told me I'd have to shake pom-poms," I said a little crossly.

"I know, and you *still* agreed to do it! Miss Mallard banned them ages ago, though. Said they restricted our arm motions and made us look ridiculous. Annabelle was furious. She was very attached to her pom-poms. And if you'd actually bothered to come and watch me cheer, you would have known that, wouldn't you?"

"Yes," I said sheepishly. Mills is right. I should have supported her better before. At least I'm doing the right thing now, although I'm not exactly over the moon at the prospect of joining the All Saints, and I'm seriously not in the mood for Annabelle's nonsense. Once upon a time I was nervous around her. Like most girls in our year, I was afraid she'd turn on me and rip me apart with her vicious mouth, but recently something inside me snapped. I'm just not prepared to kowtow to her anymore. Someone has to stand up to her or she'll boss and bully her way through the next five years of school, steamrollering over anyone who gets in her way, and that's not a pleasant thought.

I look at her now. "It's the changing rooms, Annabelle. I'm about to get changed. Just let me past."

Her eyes narrow. "There's no hockey practice this afternoon. So what exactly are you getting changed for?"

Despite my determination not to let Annabelle get to me, I gulp. When she's in full interrogation mode, she's pretty scary.

"I'm joining the All Saints," I say, trying not to let my voice quiver.

"What? Says who?"

"Miss Mallard. I'm taking Nora-May's place until her ankle's better."

"Over my dead body. Sophie, Nina, don't let Green in the door until I've spoken to the Duck." Annabelle pushes past me rudely and stomps off to find the coach. I wonder if she calls Miss Mallard "the Duck" to her face? I doubt it. No one messes with Miss Mallard, not even Annabelle.

"Come on, this is ridiculous," I say to Sophie and

Nina. "I'm actually doing you lot a favor. Without me you won't be able to do your precious Full-up Liberty at the Nationals."

"She has a point," Sophie says.

"No way. Look at the state of her," Nina says, as if I'm not there. "She's a squirt for starters."

"I am not a squirt," I say indignantly. OK, so I'm on the short side, but that's so unfair.

"She's hopeless at gym too," Nina continues, ignoring me. "And she doesn't have the right *look* to be a cheerleader." Her eyes rest on my rather flat chest and then dip to my average-size waist. "We do have standards, you know."

I'm determined not to let her get to me. "You're not in a position to be picky, Nina. I don't see girls exactly lining up to join the squad. Probably because they're afraid of all your body-police rubbish. I'm normal, get it? Normal weight, normal boobs, normal pimply teen skin. Get over yourself. And I'm joining your stupid All Saints whether you like it or not, so deal with it."

Sophie sighs. "Just let her get changed, Nina."

Nina stares at her. "Whose side are you on, Pig-face? You heard Annabelle. And I have a question, Green. If being an All Saint is so stupid, why do you want to join in the first place? Answer that."

"Because she's my best friend and she knows how important Nationals are to me," Mills says, appearing behind me. "And for your information, I am now head cheerleader, which means I get to order you two around for a change."

"What about Annabelle?" Sophie asks.

"Miss Mallard said it would be healthier to have two head cheerleaders," Mills explains. "She sent me in to tell you all to get a move on. We'll never win Nationals at this rate. We need to practice until we can do our routines in our sleep. Amy, why aren't you changed?"

"Ask your subordinates, Head Cheer," I say.

"Your *what*?" Nina snaps.

I smile at her. "Look it up. Now, are you going to step away from the door, ladies? You heard Mills — we'll never be winners unless we practice. Chop-chop!"

After glowering at me for a long moment, they both march out to join Annabelle.

"Is winding up the D4s a sport?" I ask Mills as soon as they're out of earshot. "Because we'd so make the Olympics if it was."

She laughs uneasily. "There's three of them and only two of us. Remember that."

"Excellent odds," I say with a grin. "Bring it on."

Mills groans. "Why am I beginning to think your joining the squad wasn't such a great idea?"

As soon as I get home that night, I fling my bag and jacket on the floor at the bottom of the stairs and dash up to my room to ring Clover in private.

"Yello? It's the hostess with the mostess, Miss Clover Wildgust," Clover says like she's presenting a cheesy game show.

"Clover, thank goodness you're there. SOS!"

"What's up, Beanie?"

"To cut a long story short, I've joined the All Saints to cover Mills's back — the D4s are trying to injure her — and I have to cheer at a game on Sunday. I'm going to make such a fool of myself. Joining the squad was such a dumb idea. What was I thinking? I had my first practice today and I've already forgotten all of the chants and motions." *Motions* are special cheerleading arm movements, and there are masses of them. Who knew cheering could be so complicated?

"Saving a friend from D4 bullying is never dumb, Bean Machine," Clover says. "And I may be able to help. I'll be at your place in two shakes of a lamb's tail. Find something we can use as pom-poms, Beans, old girl — Evie's cuddly toys or something. We're going to do some righteous shake-shake-shaking." She starts singing an old song about shaking your booty and then puts the phone down before I get the chance to tell her about Miss Mallard's no-pom-pom policy.

Clover is full of energy when she arrives. She bounces into my room like a fully sugared-up toddler. She's wearing a white Juicy tracksuit and pink-and-yellow Nike high-tops.

"Little Miss Fix-it at your service," she says, doing jazz hands. "Ta-da! Now, tell me about your cheer fear. I'm all ears. Shoot."

"I had no idea how complex cheering would be. I thought it was just waving a few pom-poms around. But the All Saints don't even use pom-poms anymore. Miss Mallard hates them, apparently."

"Really? They certainly used pom-poms in my day. Well, Beanie, I guess we have some practicing to do. Fire up your computer. There are bound to be some cheerleading demonstrations on YouTube."

"Why didn't I think of that?"

"Because I have the superior brain, Bean Machine."

I type CHEERLEADING DEMONSTRATIONS into YouTube and dozens of videos come up, including one that's a step-by-step guide to a successful Full-up Liberty. We watch some of the clips. The best one is of an American professional cheerleading squad called the Boston Twirlers doing a Double Full-up Liberty. It's really impressive! The Boston Twirlers have also put together some great guides on how to do arm motions, demonstrated by a girl who looks freakily like Nora-May from school.

"Lesson number one," the girl says. "Perfect your punch. You have to punch out each arm motion, like this—*bam!*" She whips her arm out. "So . . . this is the High V, the T, the Broken T, Daggers . . ."

Clover and I follow along, punching our arms as instructed.

"Hey, this is fun, Beanie," Clover says after we've been practicing along to the clips for a while. "Beats the gym any day."

"You hate the gym, Clover. You never go."

"Another hour of this and I won't need to go, ever. My upper arms will be supertoned. Yay to cheering."

My aunt really is crazier than crazy golf.

# ♥ Chapter 4

"I'm getting bad vibes from this place, Amy," Brains says as we approach the posh Royal Dublin Society Building in Ballsbridge, where the Bridal Heaven Wedding Fair is being held. Mum was supposed to come with us, but Dave, who is a nurse at Saint Vincent's Hospital, had to fill in for someone at work at the last minute, so she's stuck at home with the babies. It's probably best she didn't come. She would have been more freaked out than Brains by this place.

The railings of the Royal Dublin Society are alive with Barbie pink and white balloons, and there's a matching balloon walkway leading from the gates to the main door, complete with a red carpet. To the right of the doorway, under a small white canopy, a string quartet is playing classical music, and on either side of the entrance are two men, each holding a bow and arrow and wearing what look like giant white diapers. They've been sprayed with gold paint from head to toe, and although they're smiling, their jaws are firmly clenched. It's March, so not exactly beach weather, and they must be absolutely freezing.

"Poor dudes," Brains says. "They'll be icicles by sundown. And what's with the bows and arrows?"

"I think they're supposed to be Cupids," I say. "You know, shooting arrows of love."

Brains sings a snatch of an old song called "Stupid Cupid" under his breath.

The quartet suddenly starts playing "Here Comes the Bride," and Brains stops singing. "Amy, I can't do this," he says, his eyes darting around like he's looking for an escape route. "I'm all for marriage, but this place is smushville. I have to skedaddle. I've got an urgent band meeting that plain slipped my mind before. Tell Clover—"

"Tell Clover what?" Clover asks, appearing beside us. She's been parking the car. She slips her arm into his. "Not thinking of running off on me, were you, babes?" She kisses him firmly on the lips. When she pulls away, Brains is beaming at her like she's a Disney princess. From the very first day they met over a broken printer—he was the computer guy at the *Goss* magazine before his band, the Golden Lions, took off—he's been crazy about Clover.

"No way, José, girlfriend," he says. "You want me, you got me. Even in this spooky pink palace."

She pats his arm. "Good-o, spiffing, and all that, what?" she says, like a posh actor from a Second World War movie. "I have plans for you, Sir Lancelot. I need you to be Dave for the day. We need to get his groom's outfit settled. But first, the VIP reception. This a-way. Tally-ho." Saffy—Clover's editor on the *Goss*—has asked Clover to cover this VIP bash for a friend of hers who edits a magazine called *Irish Bride*.

Clover pulls Brains toward a smaller doorway to the left of the main entrance. It's also framed by an arch of balloons, white and silver ones this time. I catch up with them and throw Brains a sympathetic look. He just shrugs and smiles. He'd do anything for Clover.

"Do keep up, Beanie, old girl," Clover says. "The nibbles will be all wolfed down by starving wedding-dress models unless we hurry. I think most of them exist on canapés, and olives from vodka martinis."

As we make our way into a big hallway with a marble floor like a checkerboard, a girl not much older than Clover, wearing a very short black skirt and ultra-high high heels, waves a clipboard in our faces.

"I'm afraid this is a private function," she trills, giving Clover the once-over. Clover's wearing silver shorts, red tights, and black biker boots. She looks amazing, as always, but this girl clearly doesn't think she is dressed well enough for a high-class journalists' do. She isn't impressed by my outfit either. Her eyes dismiss my jeans and black-and-white stripy sweater in a second. But they linger over Brains's Afro and black-rimmed geek glasses. He may have an unusual style, but he's very handsome.

She turns back to Clover and physically winces as if she has only just caught sight of the pink stripe in Clover's white-blond hair. This girl is really rude! Clover doesn't seem in the least bit bothered, though. She shimmies around her so she can read the clipboard and then points at the top of the list. "We're right there — 'Clover Wildgust and guests, *Irish Bride.*'"

"*Irish Bride*? You seriously expect me to believe you're from *Irish Bride*? Where are your invitations, then?"

"In one of my editor's many handbags," Clover explains. "She couldn't find them, but she rang your office to change the name on the invite list. I didn't think it would be such a problem."

The girl smiles nastily. "If you're from *Irish Bride*, then I'm Lady Gaga. I'm sorry, but as I said, it's a private party. You'll have to leave."

Brains and I exchange looks. "It's no biggie, babes," he says. "It'll probably be boring anyway. Let's vamoose."

"It *is* a big deal. I told Saffy I'd make some business contacts for the *Irish Bride* advertising department. Hettie, the editor, is her best friend, and Saffy's taking her away to a spa this weekend for her birthday. I promised I'd cover this. And it's all good experience for the future."

"Why don't you show Miss Clipboard your driver's license?" I suggest. "Prove who you are."

"Genius, Beanie," Clover says, taking her wallet out of her handbag. She holds the license out to the girl.

"I'm so sorry, Ms. Wildgust," the girl says after reading the name on it. "It's just you all seem so young. Students are always trying to gate-crash our parties for the free drink. I'm sure you understand why I have to be cautious. I'm just doing my job."

"And I'm just doing mine," Clover says. "Can we go in now?"

"Yes, of course," says the girl. "Up the stairs and to the right. And please accept my apology. If there is any way you could forget about the whole misunderstanding, I'd be very grateful."

Clover smiles. "Don't worry, I don't tell tales out of school. I'm not that kind of gal." And holding her head high, she sashays past the girl. "Come on, troops, the canapés are calling."

"Love your work, Gaga." Brains gives the girl a parting wink, then hooks Clover's arm and starts belting out Lady Gaga's "Edge of Glory," his deep voice rebounding off the walls and filling the hall.

As Brains predicted, the reception is deathly boring: tall, skinny models wafting around the room in slinky wedding dresses (they probably banned the meringue kind in case they got stuck in the doorways), women in expensive-looking wrap dresses pretending to talk to each other but really checking to see if there is anyone more interesting in the room over their "friend's" shoulder. The canapés are spectacular, though. There are tiny poached eggs on toast (I nearly gag when Brains tells me they are quail eggs — after I've eaten at least three), smoked salmon blinis with tiny black dots of caviar (which I scrape off with my finger — no way am I eating fish eggs, even posh fish eggs), and my favorite — baked mini Camembert cheeses, still in their boxes, which come complete with bread sticks the size of my baby sister Evie's fingers to dip into the warm, squidgy insides. On Clover's instruction, I'm taking notes for Mum's wedding, so I jot down, "Mini Camembert boxes with teeny-weeny bread sticks, but no quail eggs!" under "Canapé Ideas."

Meanwhile, Clover is working the room like a pro, chatting to the magazine editors, and making them all nod furiously and laugh out loud. I must remember to ask her what she's talking about that is so funny. I do hear her say something about New York at one point. "That's right, in New York. We'll see what happens." Maybe she's chasing an interview with a big movie star over there. Maybe she'll take me with her? While Clover is schmoozing, Brains and I mostly hang around, testing the canapés and talking only to each other.

"These people sure know how to party," Clover says, rejoining us. "Am I right or am I right? Hell of a shindig"—she lowers her voice—"if you're an undertaker. I'm delighted to report that my work here is done. I've chatted to all the editors, soaked up some wedding-dress ideas for Sylvie, and picked up lots of advertising contacts. Let's make like a banana and split. Dare you both to zombie-walk outta here."

Brains grins. "You're on. Ghoulish girlies, let's shake an undead leg."

Clover flicks her head to the side like one of the zombies in the Michael Jackson music video. It's one of her favorites.

Brains loves it too. He starts to sing "Thriller" softly under his breath and we all put our hands out in front of us and march toward the door, with widened eyes staring vacantly into space and stiff limbs. There a few raised eyebrows, tut-tuts, and shocked laughs, but we ignore them and continue dead-marching down the stairs. Outside, we dissolve into giggles.

"How do you do that?" I ask Clover as we walk back toward the main entrance to the wedding fair, where the Cupids still stand waiting.

"Do what? My splendorific, Oscar-winning zombie impression?"

"No! Although it is impressive. Talking to those scary-looking adults. How do you know them all?"

She shrugs. "I don't."

"Really? You just went up to them and . . . said what, exactly?"

"'Hi, I'm Clover Wildgust from *Irish Bride.*' Then they introduce themselves and I start asking them questions."

"What sort of questions?"

She smiles gently. "Grown-ups are just people, Beanie. Wrinkly humans wearing yawnsville clothes, admittedly, but people all the same. I ask them about their job, their kids, where they bought their wrap dress — anything, really. And here's the important bit: I listen to them — that's the trick." She shakes herself, like a dog throwing off water after a swim. "Wowsers, that's all far too serious for this hour of the morning. All set to watch some skinny models in some blissfully bad wedding frocks frolic down that catwalk?"

"Abso-doodle-lutely!"

"Fabulous. Now we're sucking wedding diesel."

Brains and I trail behind Clover as she checks out the wedding fair. The wedding-theme fashion show is due to kick off shortly on the large catwalk that divides the huge hall. On either side of it are dozens and dozens of stalls, all pushing different wedding wares, from dresses to exotic honeymoon destinations.

Clover comes to a halt in front of a large stall with a sign saying GOOD GROOMING hanging above the unmanned table. Three male mannequins stand behind the table in different groom outfits, their waxy faces staring out at us.

"Ooh, I like that one," Clover says, pointing at the middle mannequin, which is dressed in a dark-red velvet suit.

"I can't picture Dave in velvet." I squeeze my eyes shut and try to imagine Dave in velvet. "Nope, not happening."

"Not for Dave, for Brains," Clover says.

"Is there something you're not telling me, Clover?"

"Not to get married in, you crash-test dummy, for band photographs. It's a very striking suit. Marriage is so not on the cards for a long time to come," she says. "But don't stop proposing from the stage, sweetness. It's darling," she adds quickly, winking at Brains, who is taking a closer look at the suit. "Makes a gal feel special."

Since January, Brains has been shouting out marriage proposals to Clover from the stage at Golden Lions gigs. Most people think it's all part of the show. Clover always says, "No way, José," and the women in the audience cheer — they all have big crushes on Brains.

"What do you think?" Clover asks him.

"Not really my color," he says. "But I dig the velvet."

"What about the cream-linen suit for Dave?" She points at the left-hand mannequin.

"Yuck!" I say.

Clover laughs. "Don't hold back, Bean Machine."

"Dave would hate it," I say. "It's too 'Look at me, I'm so handsome.'"

"Amy's right," says Brains. "That one would be more Dave's style." He nods at the third mannequin. "Dark-gray morning suit, nice and traditional."

"I'm so sorry I wasn't here to welcome you," says a voice behind us. "One of our male models hasn't turned up for the fashion show and I'm all in a tizzy." We turn to find a tanned man smiling at us. He's wearing a plain dark suit, and a tape measure hangs around his neck like a thin scarf.

"Not a problem," Clover tells him. "Can my boyfriend try on the gray suit, please, with a yellow vest if you have one and a sky-blue cravat? It's for my sister's wedding. We're just the organizers and Brains is our model for the day."

The man looks Brains up and down. "Model, did you say . . . ? Ladies, would you mind if I borrowed this young man for a moment. He'll meet you at the fashion show later. Here." He presses a couple of fancy white-and-gold invitations into Clover's palm. "With my compliments. And after the show we can talk about your wedding plans. I'm sure we can work out a special deal."

"Thanks," Clover says. "That's really kind of you, Mr. . . . um? But what do you need Brains for?"

"You'll see. And the name is Stanley. Noel Stanley, but please call me Stan. Everyone does." He drags a bemused-looking Brains through the curtain at the back of the stall.

"Where do you think he's taking Brains?" I ask Clover.

Clover shrugs. "To do some heavy lifting. Or to look for his missing model." She winks. "Hey, the fashion show's about to start and we have ringside seats. Chop-chop, Beanie." She's right — through the sound system a loud voice is asking people to take their seats.

The seats are amazing, right up against the catwalk. Music starts pumping out of the loudspeakers. I swivel toward the stage to watch the models sashay down the catwalk in lots of different white and cream dresses. They're all nice frocks, but nothing special. And I don't think Mum would like any of them. After we've seen about thirty dresses and ten groom and usher suits, Clover begins to slump in her seat and yawn.

"And now for the finale," a voice says over the PA system. "Our fantasy wedding couple!"

"Thanks goodness for that," Clover says, sitting up. "I can't take much more. Whatever Brains is doing, it's got to be better than this."

A bride and groom step onto the catwalk in the most amazing outfits — the willowy blond model is wearing a bloodred taffeta wedding dress, and the male model's black-velvet suit is gorgeous. Hang on, that isn't any old male . . . It's Brains! I gasp and nudge Clover, who is smiling away to herself.

"I had a feeling we might see him on that catwalk," she says.

Brains stops just in front of us. "Will you marry me, Clover Wildgust?" he asks loudly.

Clover hesitates, as if weighing up her options. For a second I think she's about to buck the trend and say yes, but instead she replies, "One day. Keep asking, babes."

At that, everyone claps and cheers.

Clover grins.

# ♥ Chapter 5

"Hey, hey, Saint John's fans, yell it out and rock the stands" may be what the rugby fans hear on Sunday morning, but in my head there's a completely different chant going on: "Cross left and kick, cross right and kick; arms in, out, in, out . . ."

"Watch your swirlies, Amy," Mills says after we finish yet another punishing set of cheers. *Swirlies* is the cheerleading term for "fists." Daft name, if you ask me, but hey, who I am to judge?

"Thumb wrapped tightly around the fingers, remember?" she says. "And keep the wrists dead straight."

"OK," I say, sucking in deep breaths to try to tame the stitch in my side.

Mills's chest isn't heaving up and down, and her cheeks are only slightly pink. She's glowing, unlike me. I am a red, sweaty mess. I hadn't realized how superfit she is. Playing goalie on the field hockey team (my usual sport of choice) clearly isn't as taxing on the lungs as cheering.

"Ready for the next cheer?" Annabelle says. "'Don't Mess with the Best'?"

I look at Mills, panicked at the thought of going straight into another set of torturous cheerleading contortions.

"Let's take five," Mills says, reading my expression perfectly. "The ref's about to blow the whistle for half-time anyway."

"Fine. But stop protecting Green," Annabelle tells her. "It's pathetic. No, *she's* pathetic. Is your jelly-belly hurting, Gweenie? Pwoor liddle Amy-damy."

I'm imagining ramming a swirlie down her smug throat when the whistle blows for half-time.

"We get another break now, right?" I whisper to Mills.

"'Fraid not. Sorry, Ames. This is when we keep the fans and the players' morale up, especially as we're losing 13–8 despite Bailey's talent. It's criminal. Bailey is ready on the wing, but Hugo just won't pass him the ball, the dunderhead."

I have no idea what she's talking about, so I just nod and murmur, "Criminal."

"You're not in your knitting circle now, girls. Stop chattering and let's get on with rallying the crowd," Annabelle snaps.

"Knitting circle," Nina says and titters. "That's a good one. Did you hear that, Sophie? Knitting circle."

"Hey, my nan's in a knitting circle," Sophie says. "And it's back in, isn't it? All that artsy-craftsy stuff."

"But your nan's, like, a hundred," says Nina.

"Shut up, the lot of you, and focus," Annabelle says. "Two rounds of 'Don't Mess with the Best' now, OK?"

After two rounds, I need to lie down. Luckily Mills says, "Let's do 'Blue, Blue, and White' next. Amy, you don't mind sitting this one out, do you? We haven't taught it to you yet."

"No," I say, giving her a grateful look. "Not at all. Knock yourselves out." I bend forward to catch my breath as the All Saints belt out another chant, thankfully without me this time.

"How was the cheering?" Dave asks as I stagger into the kitchen, flop down into a chair, and then rest my head on the table. My whole body feels like I've been pummeled by Katie Taylor, the Irish Olympic boxer.

"I have never been this exhausted in my whole entire life," I say. "Please feed me before I pass out."

Dave smiles. For some reason he's wearing Mum's pink rubber gloves with pink fake fur at the cuffs. They look pretty funny on his hairy forearms. "I just happen to have cooked lasagna for lunch. It should be ready any minute now."

That sounds promising. Dave's lasagna is surprisingly edible.

"Where are the troops?" I ask him, meaning my little brother and sister. Alex is two and a bit and Evie was one in January. I love them to bits, but, boy, are they a handful!

"I've parked Evie in front of *Peppa Pig*, and Alex is upstairs playing with a cardboard box," Dave says. "I took him to the toy shop this morning to choose a new train, but he spotted this big cardboard box and refused to leave without it."

"My bro, the cheap date. Where's Mum?"

"In bed." He lowers his voice. "She's a bit tired today, so I told her to go and lie down for a while and take it easy."

That doesn't sound good. When it comes to Mum, feeling "tired" spans a wide spectrum of emotion, from a little bit weepy to thumping pillows and wailing. Sometimes, if she's really bad, we have to ring Clover for help. Clover is the only person who can get through to Mum when she's in one of her darkest-of-Peru moods. Mum has always been a bit fragile. Sometimes I feel like I'm the parent and she's the child. Other times, though, she surprises me by being totally smart and together. This is clearly not one of those days.

"Should I ring Clover?" I ask him.

"She'll be fine. She's just a bit stressed out about the wedding. I keep telling her you girls have it all under control, but she won't listen to me."

"Of course I won't listen to you." Mum appears in the doorway with Alex on her hip.

Darn it, I should have closed the door behind me. How long has she been standing there? She looks terrible. Her hair is greasy and tied back in a messy ponytail, and she's wearing a pair of navy tracksuit bottoms and an old gray hoodie with a rip on the arm that I tried to throw out weeks ago, but she fished it out of my trash can, saying there was plenty of wear in it yet. Alex is a bit of a mess too. His face is filthy, with weird pink stains on his cheeks.

"Amy's only thirteen," she says, "and Clover's so caught up in ridiculous details like doves and cupcakes that she's overlooked the really important things like my dress and registering the wedding."

"I'll be fourteen soon," I remind her, but she doesn't even glance at me—her eyes are fixed on Dave.

"And look what Alex has done." Mum throws something at Dave and it hits his chest and then clatters to the floor. It's the stubby end of a lipstick. Ah, that would explain the streaks on Alex's face. He has a habit of stealing Mum's lipsticks and drawing with them. "You can't leave him upstairs on his own, Dave. How many times do I have to tell you? And look at this place. It's a bomb site. You've used every single pot in the house again and the stove is covered in tomato sauce. Why can't you clean up as you go along?"

"I was just about to deal with it." Dave waves his gloved hands in the air. "See? Take it easy, Sylvie. And I'm sorry about your lipstick. I'll buy you another one, OK?"

"That's not the point! And take off those gloves. They look ridiculous on you."

Alex struggles, kicking his legs, and Mum puts him down. He immediately runs under the kitchen table. "Pwison!" he shouts, rattling one of the chairs. "Pwison."

Mum pulls out the chairs, flips them over, and

puts them back on the table so that the seats are resting on the tabletop, to make a "prison."

Chuckling away to himself, Alex peeps out from between the "prison bars." "Pwison, pwison. I in pwison."

Dave and I both laugh at him, but Mum doesn't even smile.

"Sylvie?" Dave says, his voice low and calm. "Would you like something to eat? It might make you feel a bit better. You didn't have any breakfast."

She shakes her head. "I'm not hungry."

"You have to eat, pet. And Amy's starving after all that cheerleading."

Mum looks at me and her eyes soften a little. "Sorry, Amy, I forgot. How did it go? I know you were very nervous about it."

"OK, I guess. But are you all right? If you're tired, I can take the rug rats to the park or something this afternoon."

"Thought you were babysitting Gracie later?" Mum reminds me.

"I'll join Amy with our two," Dave says. "Leave you to a bit of peace and quiet, Sylvie."

"Thanks, Dave." Mum's eyes start to glisten and her lower lip wobbles. "And you're a good girl, Amy.

I'm sorry, I didn't mean to snap at you both. Things are just getting on top of me at the moment. And this stupid wedding isn't helping. There's so much to do still."

"Sylvie, let's all sit down and have lunch together and we can talk about it, yes?" Dave looks at her hopefully.

"We can't," Mum says, sniffing and rubbing away her tears with her fingers. "Alex is in prison, remember?"

"Time to escape, buddy," Dave tells Alex. "It's lunchtime. Lasagna, your favorite."

We soon get the table and chairs back to normal. Dave straps Evie and Alex into their high chairs and then puts a big plate of steaming hot lasagna in front of me. I help myself to some salad and then test a forkful of the meat — it's delicious.

"Mum . . ." I say slowly, putting my fork down to wait for everyone else to be served before I start — Mum's a stickler for table manners. "Clover really does have everything under control. Honestly. The town hall is booked for the ceremony, the Dalkey Island Lodge for the reception, the menu's all arranged, plus the car and the cake and the flowers. She even found a company at the wedding fair that will do a good deal on the suits for Dave and the ushers. And we got our bridesmaids' dresses in Paris, of course. The only big thing she hasn't settled yet is your dress, but you said you wanted to do that yourself, remember?"

Mum looks bewildered. "Did I? Are you sure?"

"Positive — it's in Clover's notes in her wedding folder."

Mum's eyes well up again. "Oh, I see . . . right. I guess I was waiting for Monique to come home so that we could go dress shopping together. But she's so busy these days. Maybe I should just get on with it alone." Monique is Mum's best friend and one of the bridesmaids, along with me and Clover. She's an actress and she's often out of the country.

"You can't go on your own, Mum. I'd love to help you pick a dress. And I'm sure Clover would too — if you'd like us to, that is."

She gives me a tiny nod. "Yes, please."

"Great. That's all settled, then. I'll talk to Clover and we'll arrange everything."

"And Sylvie," Dave adds, "we did all that registration stuff last November. You really have nothing to worry about."

"I'm sorry," Mum says, wiping away more tears. "Of course we did. I'm such an idiot. I don't know why you put up with me, Dave."

"Because I love you, Sylvie, and I always will. Which is why I want to marry you. Now let's eat before the food gets cold."

I'm just forking the last piece of lasagna into my mouth when the doorbell rings. "I'll get it," I say, jumping to my feet. "It's probably Dad."

When I swing open the door, Dad's on the doorstep, holding baby Gracie in her little Rock-a-Tot chair with one hand.

"Hi, Amy," Dad says, all smiles.

"Who is it?" Mum calls from the kitchen.

"Dad," I shout back.

"Already?"

Dad looks a bit sheepish. "Sorry, I know I'm a bit early. Shelly's keen to get moving. She's waiting for me in the car. She said to say hi. We're going shopping together in the dreaded Dundrum." Dad gives a dramatic shiver — he detests shopping.

"Lucky you," I say with a grin. "It's OK. I'm all set. I'm going to take Gracie to the park with Dave, Alex, and Evie."

"Perfect." Dad hands over the Rock-a-Tot and the changing bag. "Thanks again, Amy," he says, giving me a kiss on the cheek. "Bye, Sylvie," he calls.

Mum sticks her head around the kitchen door —

literally just her head. I don't think she wants Dad to see her dressed like a bag lady. "Bye. Have a nice afternoon."

Once Dad is out the door, she joins me in the hall to help me with Gracie's stuff. She takes the changing bag while I carry Gracie. She's getting heavy — her Rock-a-Tot is almost pulling my arm out of its socket. Once in the living room, I crouch down and unbuckle Gracie from her little seat. Then I sit on the sofa and pop her onto my knee. Mum sits down beside me and starts to stroke Gracie's mop of white-blond hair. It was strawberry blond when she was born, but it's been getting lighter and lighter every month. Dad calls her his little Nordic beauty.

"Gracie looks just like you when you were this age, Amy," Mum says, her eyes misting up a little. "She's good-natured like you were too. And she has hair like her step-aunt Clover's. It's a killer combination." She pauses. "Amy, there's something I've been meaning to say. About Clover. Now's as good a time as any."

"What?" I ask, curious.

"Clover's been offered an internship over the summer. At *Vogue*."

"She hasn't said anything to me about it," I say, miffed that Mum knows something about Clover that I don't. "*Vogue*? Wow, that's really impressive." Clover worships the *Vogue* team and has always dreamed of working on their magazine in London. "Is she going to take it?"

"She's not sure yet. She has to talk it over with Gramps and Brains."

"You mean she might actually go?" I ask. "To London, I mean."

"New York, in fact," Mum says.

I can hardly get the words out. "New York? Hang on, you're talking about *American Vogue*?" So that's what Clover was telling those editors at the wedding fair. I haven't gotten around to asking her about it yet. I probably wouldn't be having this conversation with Mum if I had.

Mum nods. "Isn't it incredible?"

"Yes, amazing." But if it's so amazing, why am I feeling all flat inside, like Coke that's lost its fizz? "When was she going to break it to me?" I ask. "At the airport?"

"Don't be like that, Amy. Nothing's definite yet. She's going to tell you when it's all decided one way or the other. She asked me not to say anything, but I wanted to give you a bit of time to get your head around the idea. I know how much she means to you. And she adores you too, Amy. She thinks you're the bee's knees."

Really? My awesome, supersmart, and Arctic-cool aunt thinks I'm the bee's knees? I'm overwhelmed and incredibly touched. A lump forms in my throat, and I swallow it back. The truth is, I don't want her to go. I know it's selfish — but how will I cope without her? She's my aunt and my best friend all rolled into one. No one can replace Clover. No one!

"Promise me you won't say anything to Clover," Mum says. "And if she does decide to go, try to be happy for her. I know you'll miss her, pet — I will too — but you can't tie someone like Clover down. She's destined for fabulous things."

"I know. And I won't say anything, I promise." I hold Gracie against me and give her a little squeeze. "Guess it might be just you and me soon, kiddo," I whisper into her hair. I'm really sad. And the one person who always cheers me up when I'm feeling low is Clover.

# ♥ Chapter 6

"Right, you lot, quiet!" Mr. Olen yells once we've all stepped off the bus outside a big old building near Saint Stephen's Green at ten o'clock on Wednesday morning. We're on a second-year school trip to a big international modern art exhibition called Emotion in Motion. As our year is large, we've been split into four groups, each with a different teacher in charge. We've got the grumpiest teacher of them all, of course — Mr. Olen. Typical!

I'm actually quite excited about the trip, but obviously I'm trying to look as bored and fed up as everyone else. It's not cool to like school trips at Saint John's.

"And try not to get run down, any of you," Mr. Olen adds. "Getting off the road might help in that regard, Stone."

"Sorry, sir." Seth steps onto the footpath.

Annabelle and Nina giggle loudly. Oh, yes. We've also had the misfortune of being landed with the pair of them. Mills and Bailey are in another group, but hopefully we'll catch up with them later. I was looking forward to spending some time with Seth on my own, but he's in a funny mood today. He's barely said a word since we left school. I've asked him if he is OK, but he just shrugs and says, "Yeah, fine. Just a bit tired."

"I want you all back in this exact spot at twelve thirty on the dot, get it?" Mr. Olen continues. "And don't think you can just bunk off and sit in the coffee shop for the next two hours. I want you to team up in twos, and I'll give each pair a work sheet to fill in. Anyone who does not hand it in later will automatically get detention, understand?"

Everyone groans.

"But, sir, what if we're, like, not interested in modern art?" Annabelle says, tossing her hair back. "I don't think we should be forced to look at, like, broken bits of toilets and stuff if we don't even do art. It's really unfair. And my parents agree, you know. They think modern art is, like, rubbish."

"Do they now?" Mr. Olen says. "So visual literacy means nothing in your household, then, no?"

Annabelle looks at him blankly.

He just sighs. "It's good for you, Annabelle. Think of it as cultural broccoli, OK? And for your information, I've seen the exhibition already and there are no broken toilets. But it's probably best to keep well away from the barbed-wire installation, and don't jump off the giant bed. I don't want any accidents."

"Sounds thrilling." Annabelle rolls her eyes. For certain teachers she turns on the charm, but Mr. Olen is not one of them. He's not important enough to bother with, in her opinion.

"Back here at twelve thirty, people, or else," he says, ignoring her. "And for God's sake, behave. You're representing the school, remember? No high jinks and no sneaking off for any reason, either alone or in couples. And that includes you, Annabelle and Hugo."

Annabelle goes bright red, then scowls at Hugo. "As if I'd go near him."

"You'd be lucky, babes," Hugo says. "So over you."

"No, so over *you*," Annabelle snaps back.

"Annabelle, enough, OK?" Mr. Olen says. "We've only just arrived and you're already giving me a headache. Right, everyone, collect your work sheets, please, and follow me."

Once we're inside the building, Seth grabs a map. We quickly peel away from the rest of the group and head for the huge white-marble staircase.

"Where first?" I ask him. "Creatures, Fear Factor, or Emotion in Motion?"

"Creatures," he says firmly. "Thataway." He starts powering up the stairs and I follow him. His legs are much longer than mine and I struggle to keep up.

"Seth! Slow down."

"Sorry." He waits for me on a small landing halfway up to the first floor and sticks out his hand. "Come on, slowpoke."

I take his hand and he pulls me up the rest of the stairs. At the top we stop to catch our breath. He drops my hand, which is a shame, but then, holding hands on a school trip is probably a bit sad.

The air up here is different. It makes my teeth feel funny, like when you accidentally bite down on tinfoil. It also stinks. "What is that smell?"

"Plaster dust?" Seth suggests.

"No, it's like chemicals or something."

Seth shrugs. "No idea. But this building was a hospital, I guess. Could be anything—bleach, antiseptic, formaldehyde . . ."

"Isn't that what they use to pickle dead bodies? I saw it on the telly once."

"Yeah, something like that. OK, we'd better start filling this in." He reads from the first page of the work sheet. "'Creatures. Question one: How does the Song Room make you feel?'"

"What's the Song Room?" I ask.

"I guess we're about to find out." He glances at the map, then points down a long white corridor. We start walking. To our right is a row of large windows, and to the left, a string of open doorways. You can walk right through some of them into the rooms beyond, but others have a red rope tied across the opening. Inside each room is a different artist's work—from colorful photos of mad-looking exotic fish to my favorite, a Ferris wheel the size of a bicycle wheel made out of Coke cans, with tiny models of endangered animals sitting in the swinging chairs. We walk into another room and the chemical smell hits us at full blast.

"I guess we've got our stink answer." Seth wrinkles up his nose. "Gross."

I look around. The back wall of the room is covered in shelves, and on each shelf are large old-fashioned glass jars topped with glass stoppers with brown rubber seals. I peer into some of the jars and then jump back when I realize what the dark-brown and purplish lumps inside are — hearts of all different shapes and sizes. Some are as tiny as an apple seed, while others are as big as a soccer ball. Below every jar is a sign telling you which animal the heart is from: bird, ape, human, cow, horse, zebra, tiger. After a few seconds the smell starts to make me feel queasy, and I go back out into the corridor. There's a bench against one of the walls, so I sit on it to wait for Seth, who's still studying the hearts. They're interesting, but also quite gruesome.

My mobile beeps as I'm waiting and I click into my text messages, glad for the distraction. AMY ARE YOU AROUND ON SAT AFTERNOON? I CAN GET A BABYSITTER IN IF YOU HAVE PLANS. X MUM

I know she needs a bit of notice to find a babysitter, so I text back immediately: SORRY, MUM, I'M BUSY ON SAT, AMY X

It's not exactly true, but I hope it will be. Seth and I haven't hung out on the weekend for ages. OK, it's probably been only a few weeks, but it seems like forever. He's just been so busy helping Polly with her photography business. I try not to be jealous — she's his mum after all — but it's hard sometimes. And it doesn't help that Mills is always blathering on about Bailey and how much they do together on the weekends.

"You OK?" Seth asks when he comes out of the room. He sits down so close that our thighs are almost touching.

I nod. "Fine. It was just the smell."

"It's pretty bad, all right. But did you check out the gecko heart? It was minuscule."

"Seth," I say before I get a chance to chicken out. "What are you doing on Saturday? Maybe we could catch a movie or something?"

"Maybe. I might have to work with Polly, though. I'll ask her later and get back to you."

"I could help too. Carry her equipment and stuff."

"There's a bit more to it than that. It's nice of you to offer, but I don't think she'll need two assistants."

"I could just watch, then, or tag along anyway." I'm starting to sound desperate. I know I should shut up, but of course I don't. "I feel like I never see you on the weekends, Seth. You're always so busy with Polly. And Mills is never around these days, what with Bailey and the cheerleading and everything."

Seth gives a laugh. "Ah, yes, the cheerleading. Won't you be busy cheering on Bailey and the other hunky rugby stars on Saturday?"

"Stop teasing me. And, no, there's no match this weekend, smarty-pants. If you're busy Saturday, what about Sunday?"

"I said I'll get back to you, all right? Stop nagging me, Amy." His voice is sharp.

I wasn't nagging him. I just want to spend some time with him — what's so bad about that? It's not like Seth to be so mean. There's definitely something up.

"Look, I'm sorry," he says. "That came out wrong. I've just got a lot of stuff on at the moment, yeah? Things will be better in a few weeks."

"A few weeks is a long time," I say, knowing as soon as the words are out of my mouth that it's the wrong thing to say. *It's not all about you, Amy Green. Just stop talking!* "It's fine, honestly," I add quickly. "I just miss hanging out with you, that's all."

He brushes some strands of hair off my face, his fingers cool against my skin. "It won't always be like this, I promise. Now's just not a good time."

I nod. "I know."

We sit there for a few seconds, staring at each other. His sky-blue eyes are soft, but there's something hidden behind them. Sadness? Worry? I'm not quite sure.

"Seth, I know there's something up. Talk to me."

He just shakes his head. "We should get on with this work sheet." After studying the map, he starts walking down the corridor. All I can do is follow him.

We end up in the Song Room. It's larger than the other rooms, at least triple the size, and you enter it through black curtains. Inside, the darkened space is circular like a drum, with a round seating area in the middle. According to the instructions on the wall outside, you're supposed to sit down, close your eyes, and open them only when the "song" starts.

So that's exactly what we do. For ages nothing happens — there's no noise at all and certainly no singing — and I begin to feel a bit silly. Finally, I hear a squeaking noise. I open my eyes.

"Sorry," Seth whispers, "just my shoes."

I shut my eyes again. And at last the audio track kicks in. But it's not like any music I've ever heard before. A high-pitched wail fills the room, followed by another. It's spooky, like something out of a horror film, and yet at the same time strangely familiar.

"Please open your eyes now," a voice says over the sound system.

When I do, boy, do I get a surprise. The room is filled with flickering blue light and two huge black shapes are moving toward us. It's just a video projected onto the wall in front of us, but it looks so real. The shapes are almost 3-D. I'm about to squeeze my eyes shut again in fright (I'm a real chicken when it comes to anything scary), when I realize what they are. Two whales. One is smaller than the other, so perhaps it's a mum with her baby. They're humpback whales, judging from their long fins and knobbly heads.

No wonder I recognized the noise. I used to have a thing about whales when I was about eight. I made Mum take whale books out of the library for me and watched endless nature programs about them. Whales are really smart animals. There was this humpback whale caught in a fishing net in San Francisco a few years ago. Divers went down to help him. It took hours because they had to cut away all the fibers caught around his fins. When he was free, the whale swam up to each diver in turn, like he was saying thank you.

I watch the screen, transfixed, as the whales swim toward me, making their loud cries. They stop, and each one seems to be looking right at us (well, at the camera, I guess). Their gaze is surprisingly soft and gentle. Then they turn and swim slowly away again. The camera follows them as they power through the water. They don't breach — flip their bodies out of the water — and nothing dramatic happens, but it's still spellbinding to watch. I'm disappointed when the film stops playing and all is quiet again. The lights come up and Seth grins at me.

"Whoa, what was all that about? Freaky."

"I loved it." I put on my best posh art-critic voice. "The art *spoke* to me, darling."

Seth laughs. "Really? What did it say exactly? No, hang on, how did it make you *feel*?" He takes a pen out of his pocket and holds it over the work sheet. "That's what Olen wants to know."

I think for a second. "At first it felt like the whales were watching us, then it was like they were inviting us to join in — to follow them . . . play with them. I suppose I felt like I *was* a whale. Swimming along with my mum, shooting the breeze. I guess 'content' would sum it up, 'happy,' even. Why aren't you writing any of this top-class art analysis down, Stone? Get with the program." I tap the work sheet.

"You seriously think that horrible noise was happy wailing?"

"Yes," I say. "Why? What did it sound like to you?"

"Doesn't matter. Your answer's better. Care to add anything else, Miss Art Critic?"

"It makes the viewer feel connected to the natural world?"

"Excellent. You're really good at this stuff."

"Thanks," I say, feeling rather pleased.

"Even if it is complete rubbish. Whales can't be happy. They're stupid sea creatures, not humans."

"Whales are not stupid, Seth. They have enormous brains. In fact, scientists think that whales and dolphins feel all kinds of emotions, like love and empathy." I tell him about the whale in San Francisco. "And I didn't say the whales in the video *were* happy," I add finally. "I said watching them and listening to them made *me* feel happy."

"Well, bully for you."

"Seth! What on earth is wrong with you today?"

"Nothing's wrong." He rubs the toe of his shoe over the floor, making that irritating noise again.

"Seth, I'm not stupid. I know there's something up. And I'm not leaving this weird room until you tell me."

Then I remember. He's been like this with me before.

"Polly," I say in a low voice. "She's sick again, isn't she?"

Polly had breast cancer last year. She had an operation and lots of treatment, and recently she's been on a new drugs trial at Dave's hospital. I thought the cancer had gone away; I thought she was better. But if she isn't, it's so unfair. She's really cool and smart, and she and Seth are mega-close. I mean, I love Mum and everything, but we're not friends like Seth and Polly are. I guess she's all the family he's got, so no wonder they're close.

"Seth?" I say again, this time in a whisper. I put my hand over his, half expecting him to pull away, but he doesn't. So I hold it, tight.

"I'm so sorry," I say. "Does she need another operation?"

"I don't know. She got the test results back only last week. They've found more bad cells in the glands under her right arm."

"What does that mean? What are the doctors planning to do?"

"I'm not sure. That's all she's said about it." He gives an unhappy shrug. "Maybe she knows more about what's going on and isn't telling me because she's trying to protect me or something. I just feel so stupid and clueless. I want to help her, but there's nothing I can do. Polly says Dr. Shine is working on a new treatment plan — she's got an appointment with her on Friday. But what if . . . ?" He stops, his voice catching.

I squeeze his hand tighter. "Seth, you can't think that way. Your mum's really strong, but she's probably finding all of this just as difficult as you are.

I'm sure she's not keeping things from you. Polly wouldn't do that. And I think you'd know if she was lying to you."

"I guess. I just . . . I want to do something. Fix things for her. All this waiting around is killing me." His hand tenses in mine. "I feel like punching something."

"I'm not surprised," I say. "It must be awful, but maybe she'll get more information on Friday."

"Maybe."

No wonder Seth has been so distracted. And I'm ashamed to say that I feel a tiny wave of relief. I thought he was losing interest in me. Then I remind myself *why* he's been so distracted, and that makes me feel terrible. How can I be worrying about whether he likes me or not when his mum is so sick?

"Seth," I say, still feeling disgusted with myself. "I really am sorry about Polly. Don't worry about doing something together this weekend if it won't work. I understand. And if there's anything I can do, tell me."

He gives a tiny laugh and bumps me with his shoulder. "Always trying to fix things, aren't you? I think you're out of luck with this one, kiddo. But thanks for the offer. And let's take a rain check on Saturday and Sunday, yeah? I'd love to hang out, but it depends on how it goes with Dr. Shine."

The whale song kicks in again, and the disembodied voice tells us to open our eyes. And we stay there, holding hands, to watch the whales again. But this time, the giant creatures' eyes don't look soft and gentle; they look sad, and I have to gulp and blink back my tears. Sometimes life is so unfair.

# ♥ Chapter 7

When I walk through the door of the kitchen after school that night, Alex is sitting in his high chair, chewing on a cookie, his mouth a sticky mess. He's even got pieces of mushy cookie in his bangs. Dave's standing in front of the stove, stirring something in a frying pan. His headphones are clamped over his ears, and he's swaying his shoulders and singing along to an old Beatles song. I sit down at the kitchen table and wait for him to notice me. His singing gets louder and louder as the chorus kicks in.

He belts the lyrics of "Let It Be" out in his strong, mellow voice. He used to be in a band — the Colts — and he loves music. He wrote all the band's songs, before he met Mum and had the babies. Now the only songs he composes are for toddlers. He's spent the last few months perfecting a show for tiny tots featuring Dinoduck—a character he's created that is half dinosaur, half duck. Dave's convinced that he's going to be the next big thing in toddler rock. Mum thinks he's delusional, but I'm not so sure. Alex and Evie adore the Dinoduck songs—"Red, Yellow, Green, Let's All Scream" and "One, Two, Tie My Shoe"—which all have an educational theme. He's had a big fluffy yellow Dinoduck costume made and everything. All he needs now is a manager, he says.

Some of his songs remind me of the All Saints cheers, in fact. Maybe working with Miss Mallard to improve our cheering repertoire could be a sideline career for him. I'm lost in these thoughts when there's an almighty roar. I jump right out of my chair before I realize that it's only Dave yelling. He pulls his headphones off.

"Jeepers, Amy! How long have you been sitting there? You nearly gave me a heart attack."

I grin. "Not long. Nice daddy-dancing, by the way."

"You weren't supposed to see that. Was it really that bad?"

"No," I lie. "You've still got the moves." The wooden spoon in his hand is dripping red sauce all over the floor. "What are you cooking? Smells strangely good."

"I'll take that as a compliment. Spaghetti Bolognese. Your mum's at the cinema with your grandpa. I'm on babysitting duty."

"Have you lost one already?" I ask, looking around the room for Evie.

"She's having a nap, smarty-pants." He puts the spoon back into the frying pan and swipes at the sticky red puddle on the tiles with a piece of paper towel — Dave's version of cleaning up. Mum would be on the floor with all kinds of sprays and wipes.

"You're home late," he says. "Your mum said you'd be back at three. It's nearly five."

I roll my eyes. "We were on a school trip, and the bus broke down. There was black smoke coming from the engine and everything. We were stuck in our seats for over an hour while the Crombies sang stupid rugby songs."

Remembering what happened next, I feel my face go red. Annabelle had this horrible, horrible idea. She decided it was a great opportunity to teach everyone on the bus the All Saints cheers. And she forced me and Nina to join in. Nina didn't need much encouragement, to be honest — she's such a show-off — but I was utterly mortified at the mere thought of waving my arms around in the aisle, let alone chanting. I wouldn't have gone along with it if she hadn't threatened to be mean to Mills.

Mills's face flashed in front of my eyes. The scared, bullied face; the face she wears when she talks about cheering.

"I'll do it, I suppose," I muttered.

And then the humiliation began. Every second of the experience was sheer torture. The worst thing was having to cheer in front of Seth. SETH! He couldn't stop laughing. It *was* good to see Seth smile, but I do wish it hadn't been at my expense.

"Rugby songs?" Dave smiles at me. "Sounds like a nightmare, all right. But at least they didn't make you cheer, eh?"

"Dave, do you still keep in touch with Polly?" I ask, to change the subject. She used to ring him with any medical questions or worries about her treatment and he'd try to help.

"Yes," he says slowly. "Why?"

I stare down at the table. I don't want to break Seth's confidence, so I can't say any more. It's good to know Dave's still looking out for her, though. "Nothing, I was just wondering."

Dave is quiet for a long time. Then he sits on the edge of the kitchen table and smiles gently at me. "Polly's in good hands, trust me. She's a really strong woman, a fighter. How's Seth doing? Is he OK?"

"He's finding things a bit difficult at the moment," I say.

"That's understandable. I know it's all a bit up in the air for them both right now. It must be hard on the lad. But at least he has you to talk to, Amy. I know all this is hard for you too and you're coping with it so well. I think you're pretty incredible, in fact. I don't know many teenagers, but if they're all like you, this country's going to be just fine."

It's one of the nicest things anyone's ever said to me. And for some reason it makes my eyes well up, which is really embarrassing.

"Thanks," I say, blinking back my tears and getting up quickly. "Just going to do my homework."

"Dinner will be ready in about half an hour," Dave says behind me. "I'll give you a yell."

I lug my schoolbag upstairs to my room. I don't actually have all that much homework because of the school trip — just a classics essay on the Parthenon (an ancient Greek temple that is actually a pretty cool building) and a couple of geography questions to answer about urban renewal in Ennis, County Clare (yawn, yawn, and triple yawn). But I'm so not in the mood.

I keep thinking about Seth and Polly and

everything. A lump forms in my throat and I gulp it back. I'm not going to cry, I'm not.

I pull my mobile out of my pocket, looking for a distraction. There's a tiny number 1 hovering over my message box, so I click on it.

YELLO, BEANIE. TELL DAVE TO KEEP ME SOME CHOW. I'M STARVING. GRAMPS IS OUT AND THERE'S NOT A CRUMB IN THE PLACE. I'LL BE OVER ANON FOR MY DIN-DINS. HAVE GOSS WORK FOR YOU TOO. CLOVER XXX

I instantly feel a little better. Clover always cheers me up. I decide then and there that I'll tell her the Bus Trip from Hell story, but I won't say anything about Polly and Seth. If I do, I know I'll only start to feel miserable again, and besides, I don't want to break Seth's confidence.

She'll laugh at the cheerleading story, though. There's no girl better to keep my mind off things than Clover Wildgust. I can't believe that she might not be around for much longer. I'll miss her so much. . . . If she does go to New York, who will cheer me up when I'm feeling blue?

"So how goes it, Bean Machine?" Clover says, coming into my room later. "Dave said you were on a school trip today. You and the lovely Sethness get a chance to slope off for some smooch a-go-go?" She puckers up her lips and makes loud kissing noises.

"It wasn't that sort of trip, believe me."

"Everything OK, Beanie Baby? You seem a little out of sorts. Not like you to be so serio-so."

"I'm just a bit tired." I say. "I had the bus trip from hell today." And I tell her all about my cheering experience.

"That sounds grimmer than the Grimm brothers," she says when I've finished. "You poor sausage. No wonder you're down. But there's nothing else worrying you, is there? It's not Seth, is it?"

"No, Seth's fine. The perfect boyfriend, as always."

"You're sure there's nothing else upsetting you?"

I'm determined not to say anything about Polly, so I shake my head.

"Honestly, just wrecked," I say firmly.

"Good-o. But remember that I'm always here for you, Beanie, if you want to talk. Day or night, 24/7. No matter where I am. *Comprende?*"

A little voice inside me suddenly says, *Ask her about New York. Ask her if she's really going. Ask her!* But I don't want to get Mum in trouble, so I keep quiet and the moment passes because she bursts into the chorus of "Ain't No Mountain High Enough," complete with elaborate arm gestures.

"This is the cheer version of the song," she says, tipping her fingers together over her head to form a mountain and swooping them down into a low *V* to form a valley.

Despite my mood, I manage to smile.

She stops singing and pulls a crumpled sheet of paper out of her bag. "Nearly forgot. Problemo for you to solve, o teen-problem guru." She hands me the letter and I smile to myself when I see my name at the top of it. First too.

Dear Amy and Clover,

I have a problem. Sorry, I should tell you my name and a bit about myself first. I'm Bethan and I live in Cavan. Recently I've started hanging out with some new friends from outside school and they're all pretty cool. Most of them are older than me. I'm 13.

My new friends have all had their first meet by now — where we live we call a kiss a "meet" — and I feel really left out. No one has been pressuring me or anything, I just feel I'm ready. There's a boy I like, Eddie, and I think he likes me too. But here's the BIG PROBLEM. I don't know how to kiss a boy or even let him know that I'd *like* to kiss him, and how can I tell when it's the right time? Is there some sort of secret message that I don't know about? Do you wink twice at a boy with your left eye or something?

I know this letter probably sounds really stupid, and everyone I've asked says it just comes naturally, but I'd really, really appreciate some factual information—a step-by-step guide to kissing.

Can you help me?

Thank you in advance,

(A very desperate) Bethan XXX


"That's exactly how I felt, remember, Clover? I asked you how to kiss Seth, and you started demonstrating by pretending to snog the back of your hand."

"And Sylvie walked in the door and caught me." Clover chuckles.

"You told her you were testing out a new lipstick."

"And she believed me. Grown-ups! They'd swallow anything." She rolls her eyes, then asks, "So what do you think? Now that you're an experienced girl of the world, care to do a step-by-step guide for Bethan? I think it'd probably work better as an article than a letter. Your very first *Goss* feature, Beanie. Coola boola."

That would be amazing! "Would Saffy really print an A-to-Z of kissing?"

"Sure, if it's good enough. It's exactly the kind of thing *Goss* fans want to read. And Bethan's letter proves it. Avoid making it too graphic, though. Don't want to offend any parental types." She puts on a New York cop accent. "Just the facts, ma'am."

"I'll do it!" I say.

"Good woman." Clover pats me on the back so hard she nearly fires me across the room.

An Ultimate Teen Guide to Kissing? That will mean lots of research. I hope Seth's up for it!

# ♥ Chapter 8

I didn't see much of Seth on Thursday, and he wasn't in school at all today, Friday. He texted me to say he was going to the hospital with Polly for her appointment with Dr. Shine. He also said that Polly isn't working tomorrow after all and promised he'd hang out with me — result! I've just texted to arrange where to meet: HOW ABOUT MCDONALD'S AT 1 AND THEN A MOVIE? THERE'S A NEW PIRATE ADVENTURE THING THAT LOOKS COOL. AND IT'S PADDY'S DAY ON SUNDAY — ARE YOU UP FOR CHECKING OUT THE FIREWORKS IN TOWN WITH MILLS AND BAILEY? XXX

OK, SURE, he texted back. MEET YOU AT MCD'S.

As soon as I spotted the word "meet," I smiled. He has no idea of my dastardly plans for him. Well, for his lips, to be strictly accurate. We'll definitely have to sit in the back row of the cinema!

On Saturday morning I get up at eleven and take a shower. In fact, the babies woke me at seven, but I managed to drift off again—Mum knew I didn't have anything on this morning and she left me to sleep, which rarely happens, so I'm already in a good mood. I dry my hair upside down to give it extra body, then tong a couple of curls into the front with my curling iron. We haven't been out anywhere, just me and Seth, for ages, and I want to look nice, so I take extra care choosing my clothes. I put on some music and start trying on loads of different outfits before settling for my denim skinny jeans, black top, and a black leather jacket of Clover's, teamed with silver Converse. I dab some lip gloss on my lips and smack them together with a satisfying *puck* noise. Now I'm ready to rock and roll!

"You look nice," Mum says as I walk into the kitchen just after twelve. "Where are you off to?"

"Just going to the cinema with Seth." An image of the two of us smooching in the back row flashes into my mind and my cheeks heat up.

Luckily Mum is too busy chasing Alex around the kitchen with a piece of damp paper towel to notice.

"What time will you be back?" she says, catching Alex. She holds him in a wrestling-style grip while she rubs his chocolate-ringed mouth and he wails in protest.

I calculate in my head. The film starts at two, and we might go for a walk or something afterward.

"Five or six, I guess," I say.

"Before six, please," she says. "And have fun."

I smile at her. "I will." She has no idea how much fun I intend to have "meeting" Seth.

I get to McDonald's at five to one and have a quick look around. Seth isn't here yet, so I sit down at a table just inside the door to wait. There's a dad with two little kids at the table beside me. They're playing with their plastic toys as he feeds them fries. Opposite me, there's a gang of D4s. I don't know them, thank goodness. They're studying their hamburger wrappers, reading out the calories and comparing them. If they're really that bothered about their weight, they should eat in a health-food café, not a burger joint. One notices me watching them and raises her overplucked eyebrows, so I quickly start fiddling with my iPhone.

"Hiya." I look up, and Seth's standing in front of me. He's wearing a creased T-shirt with an old blue zip-up hoodie over it, and his hair is limp and falling over his eyes. I feel a bit disappointed. I spent ages getting dressed, and he looks like he picked yesterday's clothes off the floor and threw them on. But at least he's here.

"Hi." I smile at him.

He smiles back, but the expression doesn't hit his eyes. My stomach tightens a little. Something's not quite right. Then I remember what he was up to yesterday — visiting the hospital with Polly. It can't have been easy. No wonder he looks tired, anxious, and a little crumpled around the edges.

"You stay here and keep the table," he says. "Big Mac meal with Fanta, yeah?"

"Thanks." I nod. He knows me so well. I take my wallet out of my pocket, but he waves it away.

"It's on me. Back in a sec." As he walks off, I notice some of the D4s' heads turn to check him out. I allow myself to feel a little smug. I bet none of them has a boyfriend as cute or as kind as Seth, even if he does look a bit of a mess today.

A few minutes later, he plunks a tray on the table and shuffles in beside me. Then he just sits there, staring at the food.

"Is everything all right, Seth?" I ask.

"Sorry, just got a lot on my mind. Let's eat." He

hands me my food, and I start to tuck in. I used to hate eating with Seth. It made me so nervous, I could barely swallow. I worried about getting sauce on my face, dropping food all over my lap, or looking like a pig in front of him. But Seth usually wolfs down his food and is a far messier eater than I am. These days I'm quite happy to eat in front of him. In fact, now I often wonder what I was fretting about in the first place. I don't think he's ever noticed how I eat.

Today Seth's eating his burger slowly, methodically almost, and instead of cramming a handful of fries into his mouth in one go, he's chewing them one by one.

"Are you not hungry?" I ask him.

He shrugs. "Not really."

"What's wrong?" I'm starting to feel uneasy again.

"Nothing."

"How was yesterday? Did you find out anything else about any new treatment plans?"

"Yeah, Dr. Shine seems to think this new American drug is a goer. Polly can start on a course of it next week. But it's going to wipe her out apparently, 'cause it's pretty strong."

"But it's good news, right?"

"Yeah, I guess so. She's going to need me around

a lot to help out. Some days she might not be able to get dressed and stuff on her own. I might have to take some time off school."

"I can help too," I say brightly. "And I'm sure Dave and Mum would be happy to —"

"We'll be fine," he cuts in quickly. "I'll manage. And she might do great. Dr. Shine said it's hard to know. The drug affects different people in different ways. They have to give her a megadose to start off with, to knock the bad cells on the head. Then once that's done, they can reduce the dose. So she won't feel sick for long hopefully. But, look, I don't really know how to say this. . . ." He tails off, looking awkward.

"Say what?"

"I need to be with Polly at the moment," he says, his voice small. "I can't . . . I can't do this, Amy."

"Do what?"

"This." He waves his hands in the air. "McDonald's, the cinema, fireworks. I need to be at home. It's not fair to you. You deserve someone who has time for you. I know you want to see more of me on the weekends and stuff, but I just can't right now. Look, I think it's best if we . . . you know . . ." He swallows. "Break up."

I can't believe what I've just heard. Is he serious? Did he really just say he wants to break up with me?

I open my mouth to say something, but nothing comes out. I just sit there in shock.

"I'm really sorry, Amy," he adds softly. "But Polly needs me."

"I need you too," I hear myself say, my heart pounding in my chest. "Don't do this, Seth. Please? I know I've been putting pressure on you to do things on the weekends, and I'm sorry, but it's OK if you can't do stuff for a while. I don't mind. We can just ring each other or something. And maybe when Polly is better, things will change. I can wait."

"You might be waiting a long time," he says, then shakes his head. "No, it's not going to work. I have to focus on Polly, and I can't if I'm worrying about upsetting you all the time. It's better this way."

"It's not better this way," I say, my voice going up a notch. "It's not! You need someone to talk to. You shouldn't have to do this on your own."

"I have to," he says simply. "I'm all she's got."

"Don't do this, Seth. Please! I'm begging you."

He drops his head into his hands, looking devastated. "I'm sorry," he whispers.

It's then that I realize he's not going to change his mind. Seth really is breaking up with me, and there's nothing I can do about it. Tears prick the back of my eyes and I feel physically sick. I press my wobbling lips together, slide out of my seat, and run from the restaurant, sensing that all the D4s are staring at me.

As soon as I get outside, I stop running and look back through the window. Seth is still sitting there, staring into space. He hasn't run after me to beg me to stop, to say he's made a huge mistake.

It's officially over. Seth Stone is no longer my boyfriend.

I have to get away from here. I head down the road toward the shopping center. As soon as I'm out of sight of the restaurant, I stop in the alleyway beside the bank and collapse with my back against the wall and dissolve into tears. I'm so upset, I don't really care who sees me, as long as it's not those D4s or Seth.

My mobile rings. It's Mills.

I click answer, but I'm too choked up to say anything.

"Amy?" she says. "Seth just rang. He's really worried about you. Where are you?"

"In Dun Laoghaire," I manage to say. "Down some alley."

"I'm in the shopping center with Mum. Can you tell me exactly where you are? I'll come and find you."

"OK." And between sniffs, I explain where I am.

When Mills arrives, I know from the look on

her face that Seth has told her everything. She puts her arms around me and gives me a hug. "I'm really sorry," she says into my hair. We stay like that until I draw away.

"I know he's worried about Polly and everything," I say, trying desperately not to cry again. "But it's so unfair!"

"I know. There's just such a lot going on at home at the moment that he can't cope." Mills sighs. "It's probably best to leave him alone for a little while, Ames, give him some space. I'm sure he'll come around in a few days when he starts to miss you. You guys are made for each other." She links her arm through mine. "Right, let's get you out of here. We can hang out at my place. Mum's still shopping, so we'll have the place to ourselves for a while."

I suppose she's right about giving Seth some space. But waiting for him to change his mind might kill me.

I let Mills walk me home, our arms linked, our shoulders bumping gently. Back at her house, she doesn't put any pressure on me: If I feel like talking, she listens; if I don't feel like talking, she doesn't force me. Either way she's there, by my side, quietly and calmly supporting me.

\* \* \*

We're sitting on her bed, and I still feel numb. I can't believe what has happened. I've finally stopped crying long enough to tell Mills about getting on at Seth to spend more time together, and about how I've started to wonder if the breakup is all my fault.

"I think I made him feel like he had to choose between me and Polly. But it's not like that. I don't mind not seeing him. I know Polly needs all his time right now. I understand that. I'm happy to stay in the background until he needs me." I pause.

"I wanted me and Seth to be more like you and Bailey," I tell her finally. "You said yourself that we're more like best friends than boyfriend and girlfriend. *Were* more like, I should say — past tense."

"I should never have said that," Mills replies. "To be honest, I guess I was a bit jealous of you guys having so much in common. Bailey and I are very different. I don't really like all that weirdy music he listens to, and . . . never tell him this, Ames . . . but I hate surfing. I like watching *him* surf, but I can't stand getting cold and the salt water ruins my hair." Despite everything, I smile to myself. Mills has beautiful hair, dark and glossy, but she is a bit obsessed with it.

As she's talking, something occurs to me. "Mills, what about Bailey? Maybe he could talk to Seth? Make him change his mind about breaking up with me."

She says reluctantly, "I'll give it a go. But do you mind if I talk to Bailey in private? Explain the situation by myself. I think I'd feel more comfortable."

"I understand," I say, even though I'd rather hear what she has to say about me and Seth.

Mills goes into the hall, and I listen to the murmur of conversation through the closed door. I can't make out anything she's saying and I feel sick with nerves, waiting for her to come back in again.

My mobile beeps and I whip it out of my pocket, praying that it's a message from Seth saying that he's changed his mind and wants to talk. But it's a text from Clover: HEY, BABES, DON'T FORGET TO FILE YOUR KISSING ARTICLE ASAP. HOPE YOUR MOVIE DATE WITH SETH WAS HOTTER THAN HOT (SYLVIE TOLD ME). GREAT RESEARCH, BABES ;) CLOVER XXX

I stare at the message, dying inside. Every word of that article will be pure torture to write now, but I still have to do it. I can't let Clover or Saffy down. I cling to the tiny sliver of hope that maybe Bailey will be able to talk Seth around . . .

The hope dies as soon as Mills reenters the room. I can tell from her expression that it's not good news.

"Bailey's over at Seth's place right now," she says. "Seth's really cut up about everything." She bites down on her lip. She's finding it hard to meet my gaze.

"He's not going to change his mind, is he, Mills?" I say, my voice a whisper. "Please tell me the truth."

She shakes her head sadly. "No. I'm so sorry."

That's it, then. Seth and I really are over. My eyes well up with tears again.

"Come here." Mills puts her arm around me and pulls me close. "It's going to be OK, Ames, I promise," she says gently. "Stay here tonight. Mum won't mind. That way you won't have to deal with your family asking you questions. We can eat ice cream and watch reruns of *America's Next Top Model*."

"Thanks. You're the best friend ever, Mills, do you know that?" I say through my tears.

"You too, Amy Green." And then she hugs me, tight.

♥ Chapter 9

Typical! Today would just have to be March 17, Saint Patrick's Day, the day the whole country goes completely crazy. Usually I get totally into the spirit of things, spraying my hair green and wearing any green clothes I can find, and then watching the big parade in Dublin city center with Mills and her parents — it's a tradition. Mum and Dave used to go every year too, but since the babies came along, Mum isn't keen. I think she's afraid that Alex will get lost in the crowd, which, knowing my little troll brother, is a real possibility.

Normally Mills and I both love giving the floats marks out of ten, and waving at the American cheerleaders, who all have green shamrocks painted on their cheeks, and singing along to the marching

bands playing "Danny Boy" and "Galway Girl."
Today, however, I can't face it. I can barely lift my
head off the pillow.

Mills's mum, Sue, sticks her head around the
bedroom door. "You guys coming to the parade? If
you are, you'll need to get your skates on. It's already
eleven and it starts at one. We need to leave here in
half an hour if we're going to find a good place to
stand."

Mills switches on her bedside light and looks
questioningly down at me. I slept on a blow-up
mattress, if "slept" is the right word. I was tossing and
turning all night, thinking about Seth, and I hardly
got a wink of sleep. I'm exhausted this morning, and
my whole body aches. I don't want to say too much
in front of Sue. I frown and shake my head at Mills,
hoping that she'll get the message.

She looks disappointed, but says brightly to her
mum, "We already have plans, Mum. But thanks for
the offer."

"Meeting the boys, are you?" Sue says. "Tell Bailey
and Seth I wish them both a very happy Saint Patrick's
Day."

"OK," Mills says. "We're going to get dressed now,
so . . ."

Sue smiles. "Of course. I'll leave you to it. See you

later, sweetheart. Back by six for dinner, please. And Bailey's welcome to join us for food if he likes."

"Thanks, Mum, I'll tell him that."

As soon as Sue has closed the door behind her, Mills gives a deep sigh. "Well, that wasn't awkward at all. Sorry about Mum. She can be a bit full-on in the mornings. Are you sure you don't want to go to the parade? It might help take your mind off things."

There's a flicker of hope in her eyes.

"There's this amazing cheerleading team from Boston over for the march," she continues. "The Boston Twirlers. They're All-American champions, apparently. Nora-May was telling me about them — her cousin's in the squad. I'm dying to see them!"

I feel bad. Mills has been so sweet to me. I don't want to stop her enjoying Paddy's Day just because I'm an emotional mess. She loves the parade, and I know she'll be disappointed to miss the Boston Twirlers. I can't believe Nora-May's cousin is in the squad. No wonder the girl in the video looked like her. If I were feeling better, I'd confess how much my cheerleading skills owe to the Boston team and their ultra-useful YouTube clips.

"I completely forgot," I say. "I promised Mum I'd help her with the babies today. You go to the parade with your parents."

"I could always babysit with you, and we could watch the parade on the telly," she offers.

"No, honestly, it's fine. We did that one year, remember, when your dad was supposedly dying from the sniffles, and it wasn't the same."

"Are you sure?"

I nod. "Yes! Now, you'd better get dressed or you'll miss the Boston Twirlers."

After we get dressed, Mills skips off into town with her parentals while I go back home, hoping Mum and Dave will have taken the babies to the park or something, so I don't have to talk to them. But who am I kidding? They're rarely dressed by lunchtime on a Sunday, let alone out of the house, and today is no different.

Realizing they are in, I let myself in the front door quietly and attempt to sneak up the stairs without being detected.

"That you, Amy?" Mum yells from the kitchen.

*Siúcra!* "Yes, Mum," I say loudly. "But I'm just going upstairs to have a shower."

"Come here first."

I sigh and walk through the kitchen doorway. Mum is leaning against the sink. Behind her, through the window, I can see Dave throwing Alex up in the air and catching him. Evie is sitting on a rug on the grass, giggling at them and clapping her hands. They look so happy, and it just makes me feel all the more sad.

"Not going to the parade with Mills and her folks?" Mum asks me.

I shake my head. "I think I'll give it a miss this year."

"Are you sick? It's not like you to miss the Paddy's parade." She reaches out a hand to touch my forehead, but I step back.

"I'm fine. I think I just need some rest. I'll be in my room if you need me." I go to leave, but she puts a hand on my shoulder.

"Amy, what's up?" she asks gently. "Did you have another fight with Mills?"

We have had two almighty falling-outs, all right, but thankfully that's all in the past, and we've both sworn that it's never going to happen again. Best friends forever.

I shake my head, pressing my lips together to stop myself from crying again. "I'm all right, Mum, honestly."

"You're clearly not. What it is, pet? Come on, you can tell me."

My bottom lip starts to wobble.

"Amy, please, you're worrying me. Is it about Clover's trip to New York? Or Polly?"

I shake my head. "No. It's Seth. We broke up."

"Oh, Amy, I'm so sorry. I'll miss him. He was such a nice lad."

"Mum! It's not about you."

She winces. "Sorry, sorry, you're right. And I know there's nothing I can say that will make things any better for you. Breakups are rough at any age. There is a pot of posh chocolate ice cream hidden behind the French fries in the freezer if that helps."

# ♥ Chapter 10

I'm sitting in my bedroom with Mills, digging a spoon into the pot of Ben & Jerry's Chocolate Fudge Brownie. It's later the same day. She came by after the parade. I couldn't face food earlier and I barely ate anything at dinner, but I feel a bit better now. And funnily enough, like Mum said, the ice cream is helping my mood a little.

My mobile beeps and I check it, telling myself it's definitely not Seth before I look at the screen (even though a tiny fairy of hope is still flickering around in my head). I was right — it's Clover. HEY, BABES, YOU'VE FILED THAT ARTICLE, RIGHT? ;)

I groan.

"Who is it?" Mills asks.

"Clover. I was supposed to write this article on kissing for the *Goss*. I'll have to tell her I can't do it. I hate letting her down, but . . ." I trail off.

Mills's eyes widen. "An article for the *Goss*? By yourself?"

I nod.

"Wow! That's amazing, Amy. Your very first solo article."

"But I can't do it."

"Why not?"

I shrug. "You know."

"Seth?"

I nod.

"Ah, Ames, writing an article for the *Goss* is a big deal. You can't let breaking up with Seth ruin things for you. Clover won't always be around to hold your hand and it's a huge opportunity to show the magazine what you can do without her help."

"What do you mean? Clover's not going anywhere." Does Mills know about New York?

"It's only a matter of time. This is Clover we're talking about — the coolest girl on the planet. Once she's got her degree, do you really think Dublin will be big enough to hold her? I bet she'll get job offers all over the world — Paris, London, New York —"

"Clover loves Dublin," I cut in quickly. "And

she loves working for the *Goss*. She's not going anywhere."

Mills goes quiet. She just sits there, gazing down at her hands. After a few seconds, she lifts her head and says, "Sometimes if you love someone, you have to let them go, Amy."

"That doesn't make any sense." But is Mills right — is Dublin too small for Clover? Does she need to spread her wings? New York would be so exciting, and in my heart, I know she'd be crazy not to take that *Vogue* internship. I wish I'd plucked up the courage to ask her about it the other night. What if she does go? What will I do without her? Especially now that I've lost Seth. I couldn't bear it if Clover left me too.

"Clover loves Dublin," I say firmly. "But it's true that the kissing article is an amazing opportunity and I don't want to let Clover down. Will you help me, Mills? Write it, I mean."

"Of course. What are friends for? At least we do know what we're talking about now."

I type THE ULTIMATE TEEN GUIDE TO SMOOCHING, BY AMY GREEN into the computer and then read it out loud to Mills.

"What about 'Kissing with Confidence' as a title?" Mills says.

I smile to myself.

That was the title I suggested to Clover a long time ago for one of her articles. I secretly wrote to her, looking for kissing advice, signing my name "Samantha." She knew it was me. "Who else would give me an idea for an article, complete with a perfect title, Beanie?" she asked me.

She never wrote the article, but she did give me valuable step-by-step smooching instructions. Only Clover could do that! God, I'm going to miss her.

"Amy? Do you like the title?"

"Sorry, yes, it's great. Nice work, Mills."

## Kissing with Confidence:
### The Ultimate Teen Guide to Smooching
by Amy Green

It's quite normal to be nervous about your first kiss (or "meet"). Whatever anyone says, it is a big deal, and it's something that you'll remember for the rest of your life — yep, even when you're old and wrinkly!

So first things first — don't kiss any old frog (or boy), just so you can say you've kissed someone. You don't want to look back and think, "Why did

I smooch that slimy swimming fan/deranged musichead/loopy skateboarder? Yuck!"

Don't rush into kissing someone just because all your friends have done it either.

If the thought of kissing someone makes you feel uncomfortable in any way, or you think you aren't ready yet, then you should wait. It's as simple as that. It's not an age thing. Some girls feel ready at twelve, for others, it's fifteen — everyone's different.

OK, so there's a guy you like. If he seems nice and the thought of getting closer to him makes you nervous but excited, you are probably ready for your first kiss.

So you feel ready for your first kiss. What next? I'm a big fan of getting to know the boy first. That way your first kiss will be special, and not just a few minutes spent locking lips with some randomer.

Some people have their first kiss at a party, others have a boyfriend for a little while before kissing him, or have a boyfriend who they never kiss. Every single person in the world is different and every first kiss is different.

So you've found a boy you like? How do you know if that boy wants to kiss you? Unfortunately, there's no secret signal! He might make it obvious by asking if he can kiss you, or he might not.

Generally if you are sitting together, just the two of you, and he's smiling, laughing, or holding your hand—flirting basically—chances are he might like to kiss you. You can encourage him by smiling and laughing back. Then he will probably lean toward you or stroke your hair and then your lips will touch for the first time.

I have to stop typing because Mills is squealing. "Can you really write that, Ames? About lips touching?" Her cheeks are bright pink.

"Mills, hasn't the penny dropped yet? We're writing a proper guide to kissing—with all the juicy details!"

She giggles nervously. "OK, but it's still a bit weird to talk about lips touching."

I smile. Mills has always been funny about things like boys and kissing. She takes it all way too seriously.

I continue:

OK, so your lips have touched, now what? Then you press your lips against his and kiss him back, keeping your lips firm and active, not floppy.

"Floppy?" Mills giggles again, but I just roll my eyes at her.

And here's a tip—most boys don't have a clue how to kiss the first time either. Here are some of the worst kind of offenders:

✱ Washing-machine boys—their tongues go around and around, and their kisses are wet!

✱ Lizard boys—their tongues flick in and out, in and out. Unpleasant!

✱ Dead tongue—they flop it into your mouth and leave it there. Yuck!

Mills is shrieking and holding her flaming cheeks in her hands now, and I'm chuckling away at her embarrassment.

"Mills, how did you ever kiss Bailey if you find the whole smooching business so mortifying?"

"It's different with Bailey. It seems natural. You know like you—" She had been about to say "you and Seth" before she stopped herself. "Sorry," she says.

"It's OK." I try to shrug off my sadness and finish the article.

How long should a kiss last? A few seconds, a few minutes—there's no set time as long as it's fun. You're not trying to set a Guinness World Record. And remember to breathe!

What happens if I do something daft, like knock his teeth with mine?

Yep, this is based on my own experience with Seth at Sophie's end-of-term party almost a year ago. But it might just help someone who is in the same awkward position. I ran off and hid in the bathroom after it happened to me, but that probably wasn't the best way to deal with it. I have a much better solution for the *Goss* readers:

Laugh it off and try again.

And here's the important bit: never do anything that makes you feel awkward or that you don't like. Ever!

Try to kiss with confidence. Pretend you know what you are doing even if you don't. And with a bit of fun practice, it will all click into place. But the truth is: The best kisses of all are kisses with a boy you really, really like and who likes you back. With the right boy, kissing can make your heart sing!

"I miss Seth," I say simply.

"I know, Ames," Mill says, giving me a hug. "And I'm so sorry." She doesn't tell me that it'll be OK or that I'll forget about him soon, and I love her for it. Because it won't be OK and I won't forget him, ever.

♥ Chapter 11

Mills and I get the train to school as usual on Tuesday (Monday was a holiday), and neither of us mentions the elephant in the car — the fact that Seth and Bailey have obviously taken a different train to avoid us, or me, to be more exact. Instead we talk about the Saint Patrick's Day parade, the Boston Twirlers (Mills says they were amazing), and me going wedding-dress shopping with Mum on Thursday evening. Clover and I are taking Mum to a swish wedding boutique called Butterfly Bridal. In fact, we talk about everything except what's really on my mind — seeing Seth again.

The first time I see him is in the corridor just outside classics. He's sitting staring down at the screen of his mobile, with his back against the wall and his head dipped. From the way his index finger is moving, I'd say he's playing a game.

Feeling my gaze, he looks up. Our eyes lock. My stomach clenches anxiously and a lump forms in my throat. He gives me a gentle smile.

"Hi, Seth," I say, just about able to get the words out.

"Hiya," he says back.

It all feels really awkward. But I miss him so much, and I desperately want to talk to him. Even just for a second. I'm about to ask him how Polly's been feeling the last few days, when Annabelle says, "Are you going inside or what, Green? You're blocking the door."

"Better go in," I tell him, ignoring Annabelle.

"See you later," he says. He doesn't get up, which implies that he has no intention of joining me, so I walk into the classroom on my own, trying to concentrate on where to sit instead of feeling sad. Normally I head for the back row beside Seth, but today is different. I don't want to spend the whole class wondering how he's feeling, desperately wanting to talk to him about Polly, about us, about anything, wanting to connect with him but knowing that I can't, that being "friends" will hurt too much. If he even wants to be friends, that is.

We're not together anymore and I have to get my head around it. Starting right now. I need to find somewhere else to sit, somewhere away from Seth Stone.

There's a spare seat in the middle row to the left of Nora-May. I drop my bag under the table and plunk myself down at it. Nora-May only started at Saint John's in November, and I don't know her all that well, but she seems nice. It turns out she *is* nice — she gives me a friendly smile.

"Hiya, Amy," she says in her strong Boston accent. "How's it going with the All Saints? Has Annabelle tried to kill you yet?"

I smile. "Not exactly. But it's only a matter of time. How's the ankle?"

"Pretty good." She sticks her right leg out and wiggles her bandaged foot up and down. "Almost back to normal. I'm off the crutches and I should be back at practice tomorrow."

I give a happy sigh. "That's a huge relief. I'm not cut out for cheering."

"Really? Miss Mallard says you're doing great."

"I think she's just being kind."

Nora-May laughs. "Think about staying on the squad anyway. If we could just get rid of Annabelle, I'm positive a lotta girls would sign up again. It's awesome fun." She lowers her voice. "You know my accident was Annabelle's fault. She was supposed to catch me, but she wasn't paying attention. She's poison, seriously."

Miss Sketchberry walks in and asks us to quiet down. It's torture sitting in class, knowing Seth is just behind me. I'm sure I can feel his eyes on my back. I force myself not to turn around to check, and I try to concentrate on what Miss Sketchberry's saying about the Elgin Marbles instead.

The week crawls by. Seth always says hi to me if we bump into each other in the corridor or outside class, but we still haven't had a proper conversation. He seems distracted in class, and I know it must be because of Polly.

Luckily the D4s are so self-obsessed that they haven't noticed we're not together anymore or they'd be picking on me like crazy. They love it when someone is feeling miserable. Maybe it's a good thing that we never held hands or smooched in school. It means our breakup is less obvious.

Mills is being sweet, hanging out with me at lunchtime and checking that I'm OK. I'm sure she'd much rather be with Bailey, especially as I'm finding it hard to laugh or even smile at the moment. But

Bailey is spending a lot of time with Seth, and I don't feel comfortable hanging out with him yet. I'm not sure if Seth would even want me around anyway. I have no idea how he feels about me now. I still don't know if he even wants to be friends. Maybe he wants to forget all about me and pretend that our relationship never happened. It's all so confusing. I'm exhausted thinking about it.

I've arranged something for Mills (with Nora-May's help) to say thank you for being such an amazing friend. I got chatting to Nora-May after class yesterday, and it turns out that her cousin from the Boston Twirlers — Mindy — is still in Dublin, staying with Nora-May's family after the Saint Patrick's Day performance. Nora-May's asked Mindy to come along to practice today to give us some tips. I've helped to arrange it with Miss Mallard.

Mills is going to be so thrilled. All week she's been talking about the Boston Twirlers and how amazing they were at the parade. I can't wait to see her face!

"I know you're up to something, Amy Green," Mills says as we walk out of the changing rooms that afternoon for All Saints practice.

"*Moi?* How could you think such a thing?" I pretend to look innocent.

We make our way into the gym, where Miss Mallard is standing with Annabelle, Sophie, Nina, and Nora-May. "There you are, girls," she says. "Now, Amy, would you like to tell the squad what you and Nora-May have lined up for them today?"

"I'd love to. Nora-May's cousin, Mindy, is in the Boston Twirlers and she's coming along to give us some pointers."

"She sure is," Nora-May adds with a grin.

"Really?" Mills squeals. "I can't believe it! Us, trained by one of the Boston Twirlers!" She starts fiddling with her high ponytail and smoothing back her hair.

"No one from the Boston Twirlers is going to be interested in you, Mills," Annabelle says. "Get a grip. And it's only one cheerleader, not the whole squad. It's hardly that exciting."

"It's still really something," Sophie says. "I saw them at the parade on Sunday, and they were awesome."

"Awesome?" Annabelle sneers. "Since when is anything *awesome*, Sophie? We're not in Boston, which is a dump of a city, by the way. It's not a trendy place to live, like New York or San Francisco."

"Annabelle, just shut it. Boston is so not a dump. You've obviously never been there." Nora-May isn't impressed. I'm not surprised. I'd be pretty annoyed if Annabelle was slagging off *my* hometown.

Miss Mallard claps her hands together. "Girls, girls, let's stop the chattering and start warming up. Mindy will be here any minute. And do me proud, girls. Remember to punch out those movements. And nice tight swirlies."

We're busy warming up when a tall, dark-haired girl who looks just like Nora-May walks into the gym. I'd recognize her from the YouTube clips even if she wasn't wearing a Boston Twirlers red-and-white tracksuit.

Mindy waves over at Nora-May, who smiles and waves back.

"Hey, everyone," Mindy says. "I guess you're the All Saints, right?"

Miss Mallard steps forward and puts out her hand. "Correct. And I'm Miss Mallard, the girls' coach. We're so delighted you could make it to our practice, Mindy. Nora-May's been telling me all about your squad, and some of the girls saw you in action at the Saint Patrick's Day parade."

"Delighted to be here," Mindy says with a grin. "Thanks for having me along. It's good to finally meet my cousin's squad. She's told me all about you guys. I'm psyched to see what you can do." I wonder if Nora-May's told her cousin that what happened to her ankle wasn't exactly an accident. I'd say she has from the way Mindy's checking each of us out. She's clearly trying to work out which one of us is Annabelle. I'm proved right when Miss Mallard introduces us and Mindy's eyes linger on Annabelle.

"That girl can't be your cousin," Annabelle hisses at Nora-May while Mindy is asking Miss Mallard some questions about our training routine. "She's white."

"My dad's Chinese–American, but my mom's Irish–American. And so is *her* brother, Mindy's dad. Is my ethnic background a problem for you?" Nora-May snaps. "Because this is an international school, and it has a strict policy on things like that."

Annabelle scowls. "No! Of course not. I was just saying—"

"Girls, please stop the whispering," Miss Mallard interrupts. "Mindy's here to give us some help." She claps her hands together. "Let's show her what we've got. We'll start with a couple of cheers, girls, and then a Full-up Liberty. We'd be very grateful for any pointers, Mindy."

"Sure thing," Mindy says easily.

After lining up, we break into a round of "Hey, hey, Saint John's fans, yell it out and rock the stands" followed by "Don't Mess with the Best."

"That was awesome, girls," Mindy says, when we've finished our cheers. "Nice work. But remember to keep those motions nice and sharp. And, girl in the middle, with the curly blond hair — Annabelle, yes?"

Annabelle stands up straighter and smiles. She's obviously been expecting the praise. "Yes. Annabelle Hamilton. Head cheerleader."

"With Mills," I point out, but Annabelle just ignores me.

"Right, Annabelle," Mindy says, "you gotta watch those elbows. They're dropping. Keep 'em nice and high. Big toothy smile, though. Must have cost ya."

Annabelle beams at the comment on her smile. "Thanks." She has annoyingly perfect teeth. I don't think Mindy meant it as a compliment.

"OK, let's see your Full-up Liberty," Mindy continues. "Impress me, girls."

Miss Mallard nods. "OK, All Saints, get into position for a Full-up Liberty, please. And Annabelle, do try to focus this time. We don't want any more accidents."

"That wasn't my fault, miss," Annabelle says. "Nora-May's too heavy to be flier. Mills is too. I think you should pick someone lighter — like me, for example."

"What do you think, Mindy?" Miss Mallard asks her. "Is weight an important factor?"

Mindy shrugs. "Sure, but it's mainly about balance. Maybe each of the girls should try out the different roles and see which one suits them best. Not everyone's cut out for flier."

"I definitely am," Annabelle says. "I'm the most experienced cheerleader here."

"Apart from Nora-May," I point out.

Nora-May smiles at me gratefully.

"My cousin is pretty talented, all right," Mindy says, winking at Nora-May. "And she has been cheering for years. But you go for it, Annabelle. Nothing wrong with a bit of confidence. As long as you have the talent to back it up. I hope you have a good backstop, though. Don't want any accidents today, do we?"

There's an edge to her voice. I don't think Mindy likes Annabelle very much. And after what she did to Nora-May, I don't blame her.

Annabelle goes red. "No . . . of course not," she says.

Mills is biting her lip. I can tell she's disappointed. I know how much she wants to be flier. But as usual,

Annabelle gets her way. Maybe Mills will get a chance later when we swap positions.

Miss Mallard claps her hands again. "Into formation, please. And Annabelle, as Mindy has suggested it, you can try flier first. Mills, backstop, please — I know I can trust you."

"But, miss!" Annabelle protests. "Mills has never done backstop."

Miss Mallard looks at her. "Would you prefer to swap?"

"No, it's fine," Annabelle mutters.

"Amy, Nina, and Sophie, you girls are on base," Miss Mallard adds.

"Nora-May can take my place, miss," I say quickly. "I don't mind. Her ankle's almost better now."

"Are you sure you'll be all right, Nora-May?" Miss Mallard asks.

"Yes, miss." Nora-May nods eagerly. "My ankle's completely healed. Thanks, Amy."

"Oh, my pleasure," I say, meaning every word. I am more than happy just to watch — forever. Now that Nora-May is back, I'm hoping this practice will be my very last brush with cheerleading.

Nora-May forms a triangle with Nina and Sophie by putting her arms around their shoulders. Then they all bend their legs. They hold their hands palms up so that Annabelle can step onto them. Then once Annabelle is in position, they straighten their legs and backs until she is level with their waists.

"You're much heavier than Mills or Nora-May, Annabelle," Sophie says. "I hope we don't drop you."

"You'd better not," Annabelle snaps. "Get on with it. And make me look good in front of Mindy, understand?"

Next comes the hard bit. The three girls will have to push Annabelle up into the air using their arms. She's already wobbling around a lot. Mills is standing behind the group, watching her carefully. If she falls, it's Mills's job to catch her.

"Lock those legs, Annabelle," Miss Mallard says. "Concentrate and stay still, for heaven's sake. Keep your balance. OK, on three, girls, lift Annabelle. One, two, three . . ."

"Nice, girls," Mindy says. "Now, keep your base strong and steady for Annabelle."

They raise her beautifully into the air, and for a split second, Annabelle stands aloft, looking annoyingly smug, her arms in a perfect High V. But then she lurches sideways. "Help!" she yells as she completely loses her balance and falls backward.

Luckily Mills is prepared. She puts her arms out. Annabelle hits Mills in the chest. Mills gives a loud "oof!" then bends her knees to take the strain. She holds on tightly, though, and brings Annabelle safely to the ground.

"Good catch," Mindy says.

"Oh, indeed. Well done, Mills!" Miss Mallard shouts. "Bravo! Are you both all right?"

"Fine," Mills says shakily.

"Yes, miss. I just lost my balance." Annabelle looks pale and shocked. Falling like that must have given her a fright. She could have sprained an ankle like Nora-May, or worse. No wonder she's so pale. She hasn't said thank you to Mills for saving her, though.

"Would you like to try again, Annabelle?" Miss Mallard asks. "Get straight back on the horse and all that?"

She winces. "I don't think so. Best leave it to Mills or Nora-May. They're better at it than me."

Hang on — did Annabelle Hamilton just admit that she's not perfect? She really must be in shock!

Mills and I exchange looks.

"You should have dropped her," I whisper into her ear, only half joking.

She shrugs and gives me a smile. "What can I say? I'm too nice."

I bump her shoulder with mine. "I know. That's why you're my best friend. My own personal backstop. Ready to catch me, no matter what."

She laughs. "That's me."

"Want to give flier a go, Nora-May?" Miss Mallard asks her.

"No, I'm on base," Nora-May says. "Mills is the best flier we've got. Mindy, wait till you see her. She's brilliant."

Mills blushes. "Thanks, Nora-May."

"Go for it, Mills," Mindy says. "Ace backstop *and* flier. Not many cheerleaders can do both. I'm impressed."

Mills's cheeks go even pinker, but I can tell that she's delighted.

My work here is done.

♥ Chapter 12

As soon as I walk into Butterfly Bridal on Thursday with Mum and Clover, I know it's going to be a long evening. I've never seen so many wedding dresses in one place in my life—dozens and dozens of them, all hanging on two ultra-long rails that run the length of the shop. Plus, the room is so white, it's already giving me a headache. Walls, mirror frames, sofa, desk, carpet, computer, and, of course, wedding dresses—all bright, blinding white. They should offer visitors sunglasses. I sigh inwardly. I've had a rotten day in school, spent trying to avoid Seth so I don't get upset, and I'm not exactly looking forward to being all chirpy and wedding-y.

"Is it just me or have we walked into a snowstorm, Beanie?" Clover whispers. It's also the kind of place where you feel you have to lower your voice, like in a church.

"Nope, it really is blizzard a-go-go," I say. "But the romantic music's a nice touch." The sound system is playing "My Heart Will Go On," the theme song from *Titanic*.

Mum hasn't moved since we entered the shop. She's still standing in the middle of the white carpet, blinking rapidly.

"You OK, sis?" Clover asks her.

Mum nods, still looking a little bewildered. "Gosh, there are a lot of dresses, aren't there, girls?"

A woman walks through the white velvet curtain at the back of the shop. She's tall and slim, with long ash-blond hair and a small, perfectly oval face. She looks like an old-fashioned doll. There's a slash of dark-pink lipstick on her full lips, and she's wearing — guess what! — white from head to toe. A classy white cap-sleeve dress teamed with neat white kitten heels. Clover's also looking smart in sunny-yellow woolen shorts, with a short black jacket, black tights, and Chelsea boots. Mum's made an effort too, wearing fitted black trousers and her good cream raincoat that she rarely wears these days on account of the babies and their sticky hands. Yikes! I feel completely underdressed in my skinny jeans.

"Good evening," the woman says politely. "Have you made an appointment?"

"Yes," Clover says firmly. "Sylvie Wildgust and bridesmaids. Well, two out of three. Monique's running late, but she'll be here soon." We're lucky Monique is available at all. She's flying back to London tomorrow morning, which is why we're here tonight and not on the weekend. Luckily, Butterfly Bridal stays open late on Thursday.

The woman smiles. "Of course, the Wildgust party. Lovely. I'm Cassandra, and I'll be assisting you this evening. Let me just check my notes." She strides toward the desk and stares at the computer screen. "Ah, yes, I remember. Sylvie is the bride. Welcome, Sylvie." She smiles at Mum. "And your wedding is on Tuesday, April thirtieth, is that correct?"

Clover and I both look at Mum, waiting for her to respond, but she still seems a bit shell-shocked and doesn't answer, so Clover says, "That's right."

Cassandra tut-tuts. "We're cutting it a little close, ladies. Most of our clients select their wedding gown at least six months before the wedding."

"But what if they change their minds about the dress?" Clover asks. "Six months is a long time."

Cassandra frowns. "Our ladies seldom change their minds, my dear. You see, at Butterfly Bridal, we believe that there is a perfect gown for every bride. Their second perfect match, so to speak." She gives a tinkling laugh. "And that's why I'm here this evening, to ensure that Sylvie finds her dream dress."

Mum finally wakes up. "Dream dress? That sounds nice."

"So, Sylvie," Cassandra says, gesturing at the comfy-looking white sofa. "Why don't you settle yourself here while we have a little chat about your vision for your wedding dress — bodice shape, fullness of the skirt, sleeves, neckline, train, et cetera, et cetera. It will give me some idea as to what gowns to show you first."

Mum looks bewildered again.

"We do have a folder of wedding-dress ideas," I pipe up quickly. "Magazine clippings."

"Excellent," Cassandra says. "Let's have a peek, shall we? And we can a flip through the Butterfly Bridal folder also. Do take a seat, Sylvie."

Cassandra fetches a large photo album with a white padded-leather cover and sits down on the sofa beside Mum with the album on her knee. Clover squeezes in beside Cassandra, holding our own wedding-dress folder, and I slot in next to Mum. It's a tight squeeze.

"Lovely," Cassandra says, but she doesn't sound all

that thrilled. I'm not sure she's used to the bridesmaids taking such an active role in the dress selection. After lifting up her album, she flattens down the front of her dress with her hands and says with a purr, "So, let's have a look at your clippings, Sylvie."

"Well, they're more Clover's ideas, really," Mum admits. "She's planning most of the wedding."

Cassandra smiles at Mum. "A wedding planner, how sensible. Shame she couldn't be here this evening."

Clover gives a cough. "Hello? Ace wedding planner at your service. I'm Sylvie's sister, Clover. We thought we'd keep it in the family."

"I see," Cassandra says slowly. "I'm sure it will all go swimmingly." She doesn't sound at all convinced, though. I suppose Clover is probably a lot younger than the average wedding planner.

Clover glares at Cassandra. She opens her mouth to say something, so I speedily jump in.

"This is my favorite," I say, pulling a random clipping out of our folder. It turns out to be a photo of a blond woman with a generous chest running through a field of corn, wearing what can only be described as a white circus tent—the skirt of the dress is gigantic.

"Really?" Cassandra frowns again. "Sylvie's a lot

slighter than that model. I'd advise something less puffy, with more classic lines. Like this, perhaps. The 'Alicia.'" She opens her own album and points at a photograph in which a tall, elegant woman is wearing a sweeping Grecian-column dress with elaborate, blingy jewel decoration sewn around the waist and neckline. It's very footballers' wives and so unlike anything Mum would choose, I can't help but start giggling.

"Maybe not," Mum says, throwing me an "Amy, please behave" look. "It's not really me."

"What about this one?" Clover pulls another image out of our folder. It's a dark-haired model this time and she's wearing a simple, fresh lace dress with a long flowing skirt. It's really pretty and I think it would look amazing on Mum.

But Cassandra has other ideas. "It's rather dated-looking, don't you think, Sylvie? Lace?" She wrinkles up her button nose. "So last year. No, I'm thinking more along the lines of this beauty. The 'Celtic Princess.'" She gives a dreamy sigh as she points at another photograph. The bodice is tight and embellished with embroidery and crystals in swirling Celtic patterns, while the skirt billows out from the knee area in a riot of white net that is also embroidered with Celtic symbols.

"That's not a dress," Clover says. "That's a whole performance of Riverdance."

I'm about to start giggling again, when I spot Mum's face. She's staring at the photograph, mesmerized.

"Do you really think a dress like that would suit me?" she asks Cassandra.

"With your neat figure, absolutely. Isn't it dreamy? I'll let you in on a secret—it's on my wish list too. Would you like to try it on?"

"What do you think, sis?" Mum asks Clover.

Clover hesitates. "If you like it, Sylvie, that's all that matters. Why don't you try on a few different styles and see which one you like the best? There's no rush and you don't have to decide this evening."

"Good idea." Mum jumps to her feet. She's fully awake now. "I'm a size six to eight, Cassandra. Do you have the 'Celtic Princess' in my size?"

"Of course, we have a sample dress for you to try on and then we order a brand-new one, which will be adapted to fit you like a glove if it doesn't already. It's all part of the Butterfly Bridal service. We want you to look your absolute best. We always say, a beautiful bride is a happy bride. Why don't we select four or five different styles, including the 'Celtic Princess' and present a mini wedding fashion show for your sisters?"

Mum laughs. "Amy's my daughter."

"Silly me," Cassandra says. "But you look so young, Sylvie."

Clover gags. Luckily Cassandra doesn't notice.

As soon as Mum has followed Cassandra through the white velvet curtain to the changing room, Clover says, "Did you hear that Cassandra woman buttering Sylvie up? *You look so young, Sylvie. You have an amazing figure, Sylvie.* What's the bet that the 'Celtic Princess' is the most expensive dress in the whole darn shop? What is Sylvie thinking?" She continues in a low voice: "All those sparkles and the fish-tail skirt. It'll swamp her. I was talking to Hettie about wedding dresses — you know, Saffy's friend who edits *Irish Bride* — and she says that when the bride walks down the aisle, you want people to say, 'Doesn't she look amazing?' not 'Isn't that an amazing dress?' Do you get the difference, Beanie?"

I'm not sure I do, to be honest, but I say yes anyway. Clover seems very riled up and I want to keep her calm. If Mum has her heart set on this "Celtic Princess" dress, we'll both have to go along with it. It is *her* wedding after all!

"They could be a while, Beanie, so we might as well do some work." Clover settles herself on the sofa, rummages in her bag, and then hands me a sheet of printed paper. "This came in today. What do you think?"

I start to read the problem letter:

Dear Clover and Amy,

I wonder if you can help me. My name is Lia and I'm 12¾. I'm off to secondary school in September (Woodbrook Comprehensive), and I'm already really nervous. None of my friends from Sixth Class are going — most of them are off to Saint Andrew's or Wesley. So I won't know anybody.

My current school has a uniform, so I don't have to worry about picking an outfit every morning. But the new school doesn't. I don't have all that many clothes, to be honest. I don't really know what suits me or what kind of things to buy, so I end up in the same old jeans-and-hoodie combo most of the time.

I know this may sound stupid, but how do you know what suits you? None of my friends are into clothes or shopping, and my mum's not that kind of person either, so I don't have anyone to ask.

I really want to have my own style, my own

special look. I think this will make me more comfortable on my first day of school and help me feel less shy.

Do you have any fashion tips? Or shop suggestions? I'd be so grateful for any help you can give me. If you have time, maybe you could even take me shopping. . . .

Best wishes,

Lia, Monkstown

I look up from the letter and smile at Clover. This is an easy one. "You told Lia you'd take her shopping, didn't you? Give her some hands-on style tips."

Clover grins. "Got it in one, Beanie. Sometimes I think you can read my mind. But you're coming too, my friend. It'll have to be in a couple of weeks, though. I'm afraid I'm up to my tonsils before that."

"Perfect."

"Speaking of perfect." She lowers her voice. "Or maybe not so perfect." Mum is swishing through the velvet curtain in a dress not unlike the one in the first clipping I pulled out of our folder — a big white meringue of a dress with an off-the-shoulder bodice and a puffy ballerina skirt.

"Dress number one," Cassandra says in a clipped fashion-show voice. "The 'Angelica.' What do you think, girls?"

It does nothing for Mum. In fact, it makes her hips look big, and the bodice is slipping off her chest.

I wince and Clover shakes her head. "The Dublin jury is not impressed, I'm afraid, Sylvie. *Nil points.*"

Next Mum appears in an ivory-lace dress with cap sleeves and a rather odd high neckline at the back. For some reason the bodice reminds me of a Spanish matador's jacket. The sweeping skirt is nice, though, very delicate.

But Cassandra tut-tuts. "As I suspected, lace is not very flattering on you, Sylvie. It definitely ages you. Let's try another style."

The next dress — the "Eliza," a white-silk sheath with a drape of material at the front and back, and a material rose on the waist — is nice but nothing special. Meanwhile, gown number four — a pale-coffee-colored number with two spaghetti straps on each shoulder and a frothy layered skirt — is wrong on so many levels. Clover sums it up nicely.

"You look like a cappuccino, Sylvie!" she shrieks. "Take it off, quick, before someone drinks you."

"Don't hold back, Clover," Mum says with a grin.

"I do admire your honesty, Clover," Cassandra

says, her carefully plucked eyebrows lifting. "Brides need someone they can trust, don't they, Sylvie?"

"You can certainly trust Clover to speak her mind," Mum says.

Monique bustles through the front door of the shop while Mum is changing yet again. "I am so sorry, girls." She gives us a kiss on each cheek. Her lips feel cool against my skin and her perfume smells dark and exotic. "I am most dreadfully late," she adds in her delicious French accent, settling her black bob behind her ears with her fingers. "I got caught on the phone with my agent, and you know how it is. Chat, chat, chat." She waves both hands in the air as she speaks.

"You look *wunderbar*, Monique," Clover says admiringly. And she's right. Monique looks extraordinary. She's wearing a cherry-red woolen cape over a black polo neck and neat black cigarette pants teamed with teetering red stilettos, which make her look even taller than she already is. With her customary slash of red lipstick, she looks every inch the superstar.

There's a squeak of delight from the back of the room. "Monny!" Mum cries. "What do you think? Isn't it dreamy?"

Mum is wearing the "Celtic Princess," or should I say the "Celtic Princess" is wearing Mum. I now get what Clover was saying—with all the sparkles and embroidery, you barely even notice Mum.

"That dress is certainly something," Monique says. She looks at Clover and then me, and we both shrug.

Mum does a twirl in front of the mirror. Then she sighs.

"It's frightfully expensive," she says. "But if we cut back a bit on other things, like a wedding car and the flowers, I think we can just about afford it. Now, Clover, I want your honest opinion. Is this the dress for me or not?"

"Does it make you feel special, Sylvie?" Clover asks carefully.

"Oh, yes!" Mum says emphatically. "Monique, what do you think?" She looks at her best friend.

Monique's eyes are welling up. It takes a lot to make Monique cry—she's pretty tough. "Sylvie, you really are getting married, my dearest friend. Ooh-la-la." She wipes away a tear. "I don't care much for wedding gowns, so I'm not the right girl to ask. But look at your face, you seem so 'appy."

"I guess that's a yes." Mum turns toward me. "Amy?"

I say what I know she wants to hear. "It's lovely, Mum. Very striking." She holds my gaze for a second too long and then collapses on the sofa beside me and puts her head on my shoulder.

"But I can't do it. I can't spend all our money on a dress. It isn't right." She takes one more look in the mirror and gives an enormous sigh. "No," she says to her reflection. "I just can't do it."

"Are you sure, Sylvie?" Clover says. "There are plenty of other dresses here, less elaborate ones."

Mum sighs. "My mind's made up. I love this dress, but I simply can't justify it. And I didn't like any of the other dresses very much. Sorry for wasting everyone's time."

"If you love the dress so much, maybe one of your bridesmaids could talk you around," Cassandra says, looking at Clover pointedly.

But Clover's having none of it.

"No, when Sylvie makes her mind up, that's that. Sorry, Cassandra. I guess my sis won't be a Butterfly Bride after all."

I don't think Cassandra is very happy. She's glaring at Clover and me as if the whole thing is our fault.

"Let me 'elp you take the dress off, Sylvie," Monique says, leading Mum toward the changing room by the elbow. "And then we will go for dinner, yes? I want to 'ear all your news."

"Thank goodness for that, Beanie," Clover says to me as we wait for Mum outside the shop. Cassandra was scowling at us both so much that we decided it was best not to stay in the white palace a minute longer. "That 'Celtic Princess' thing was hideous."

I laugh. "I know. But what are we going to do now? Mum still doesn't have a wedding dress."

"We'll think of something, Beanie, never fear. The perfect dress is out there waiting for her, you'll see."

♥ Chapter 13

Just over a week later, on Friday night, I get a text out of the blue: WHY ARE YOU IGNORING ME, AMY?

Seth!

How dare he! Ignoring him? My head races with confused thoughts. Hang on, he broke up with me, not the other way around. He has no right to accuse me of ignoring him. I'm just keeping out of his way. Seeing him and talking to him hurts too much. Plus, I have no idea where I stand. Does he even want to be friends? I still have no clue. This is the first time since we broke up that he's said anything to me other than hi. What did he expect me to do?

After a few minutes, I start to have another thought. Does Seth want to get back together? Is that it? Mills said he'd change his mind, but I hadn't dared hope for such a thing. But maybe . . . maybe . . .

I grab my mobile and press in his name, my heart racing.

"Amy?" He sounds relieved. "Are you talking to me again?"

I practically dissolve into tears on the spot. Seth and I haven't spoken on the phone since we split up, and it almost breaks my heart to hear his voice again, all soft and anxious.

"What are you talking about?" I say. "You broke up with me, Seth. And OK, yes, I've been avoiding you a bit." I take a deep breath. "It's hard. Seeing you. In school, I mean. I can't—" I break off before I start to cry. "I'm sorry."

"I understand. It's hard for me too. But please don't shut me out, Amy. I know I've hurt you, but I miss talking to you so much. Can't we be friends or something? Please?"

I give a strangled laugh. Friends? So he *does* want to be friends. But why is he asking this right now? I don't understand and I don't know what to say, so I say nothing.

"OK, maybe not friends," he adds quickly, "but can we at least speak to each other?"

I really miss our chats too. It's like part of me isn't there anymore. So even though everything in my being screams, *Say no. This is a very, very bad idea*, I sigh, then say, "I guess." I suppose that, despite everything that has happened, I'm still clinging to the faint hope that he'll change his mind. That he'll love me again.

"Cool. Thanks."

There's an awkward pause. Then I ask, "How's Polly? How's the treatment going?"

"The new drug seems to be suiting her OK. There don't appear to be any major side effects so far."

"That's good, right?"

"Yeah, but she's pretty tired. And she's not eating much."

"And what about you? Are you eating?"

He laughs. "You sound like Polly. I'm fine. Worried about her, I suppose, but yeah, I'm eating."

"Of course you're worried, but Polly's strong, Seth. She's going to be all right."

"I hope so. Thanks, Amy."

"For what?"

"For listening. I'd better go now, check on Polly. Um, bye." But he doesn't hang up for ages. He just stays there and I can hear the faint noise of his breathing down the line. Eventually I whisper, "Bye, Seth," and switch off my mobile. Then I start to cry. I miss him so much.

What is all this about? Is he really starting to change his mind? I wipe away my tears, wondering if it could possibly be true. I guess everyone's right. I just have to give him time. All this waiting around is slowly killing me, though.

The following day is Easter Saturday and it's time for Dave and Alex to be fitted for their wedding suits. Clover can't make it, as she has a hot date with Brains. She's really busy these days, what with juggling Brains, college, and her *Goss* work, and I hardly get to see her anymore. She has been really sweet since my breakup with Seth, however, sending me THINKING OF YOU, BEANIE, and CHIN UP, BABES texts every few days, as well as funny YouTube clips of tiny micro pigs climbing out of tea cups and things like that. Today she's delegated the task of helping the groom and his mini-groomsman, Alex, to me. Dave's decided to have two best men, Dan and Russ. Annoyingly, neither of them can make it today. They are going to get fitted next week instead.

I still keep thinking about Seth, so I'm glad of the distraction. I was hoping to talk to Mills this morning about Seth's phone call, but she's cheering at the Nationals. It's in Navan, and they had to leave really early. She asked me to come with her, but I'd already promised Clover I'd be on wedding duty. I hope they win. They certainly deserve to.

Good Grooming is in Monkstown. We park the car and walk toward the shop, Dave and I swinging Alex by the arms between us. Alex loves soaring into the air and is giving happy shrieks and squealing, "More, more!"

Stan is there to greet us when we arrive at the shop. He is super-nice to Dave and Alex, even giving Alex tiny chocolate eggs to keep him quiet while Dave tries on his suit. When Stan asks Alex how old he is, Alex puts up three fingers.

I smile. "Alex, you're two and a bit, not three."

He scowls at me. "I big boy. I three."

"Ach, you look at least three to me," Stan says. Alex puffs out this chest. "I'll just take a few measurements and then we'll see what we have for you in the big boy section. And then will you try it on for me? Show everyone how grown-up you look?"

Alex nods solemnly.

Stan takes his measurements and then picks out a mini-suit for him to try on. A few minutes later, Alex struts back through the changing-room curtains like a child star. He looks so cute in the teeny black tailed jacket and gray flannel trousers.

I give a happy sigh. "Mum's going to love it."

"Doesn't he look fab-a-lous?" Stan says.

I whip out my iPhone, line Dave and Alex up on the screen, and then click. The image is captured. Dave standing tall and proud, and Alex . . . with his finger up his nose.

"Alex!" I say, giggling. I take another shot — this time without the nose-picking.

On the way home we stop for some lunch in Gourmet Burger on the seafront in Dun Laoghaire.

"Special treat," Dave says. "Are you sure you don't have any plans today, Amy? I'm not making you late for anything?"

"No, no plans." *Since Seth has abandoned me,* I feel like adding, but I don't. I'm still confused about last night's conversation. But I'm trying not to think about it too much.

After we've ordered our food — a kid's burger for Alex, a Manhattan for Dave (with two burgers — he must be hungry), and a cheeseburger for me — Alex attacks the coloring sheet with stubby markers, and I gaze out of the window at the passersby. The sky is gray and cloudy, but at least it's not raining. Oops, no, I was wrong. Plump raindrops are just starting to splatter the glass, and the people outside are dashing for cover.

"Penny for them," Dave says.

"Sorry?" I ask, confused.

"Your thoughts. You looked like you were mulling something over."

"Not really. Just people-watching."

"Stan was nice, wasn't he? He was surprisingly quick too. I thought we'd be there for ages. I bet it was a lot different from your Butterfly Bridal trip. Sylvie told me about some of the crazy dresses."

I smile. "A bit different, all right." That reminds me, Mum still hasn't found a dress yet, which is slightly worrying. I must talk to Clover. It's getting kind of urgent.

"Good to see you smiling, pet. I know things are difficult for you at the moment, what with Seth and everything. But I guess you don't really want to talk about it."

"No."

"Fair enough. But if you do, I'm here, OK?"

I nod silently.

Dave's eyes are soft and kind. "Are you sure you're all right, Amy? Sometimes talking can help."

I gulp, feeling a little overwhelmed and teary

again. I'm about to say, "I'm fine," when I think, actually, no, I'm not going to lie to Dave. He deserves to know the truth. And I really need to share this with someone.

"I miss him so much," I say instead. "We were a team, you know? Seeing him in school every day is hard. He rang me last night and asked if we could be friends. I don't get it. He wants me in his life but not as his girlfriend. It doesn't make sense. Do you think he's changing his mind, Dave? Do you think he wants us to get back together? Is that why he rang? You were a boy once. How do boys think?"

He smiles gently. "I was. Seems like a long time ago now. Well, I guess sometimes boys can think about only one thing at a time, so they shut everything else out. I'm sure he rang because you understand him more than anyone else does and he wanted to talk. You guys were very close, and all the stuff with Polly . . ." He shrugs. "You get it. You're a good listener, Amy. And my honest opinion? Yes, I think he probably will change his mind once Polly's back on track."

"Do you really think there's a chance we'll get back together? You're not just saying that?"

"Yes," he says simply. "I do. Just give him time."

"Thanks, Dave." I smile at him, my heart suddenly light.

"Any time, pet. And I'm always here if you want to talk, yeah? I know we had our ups and downs at the start, but I'd like to think we're friends now."

Dave's right about our "ups and downs." I found it difficult to have him around at first—I didn't want anyone taking Dad's place, so I made it hard for Dave when he first moved in with us. But now it's like he's always been part of the family. OK, it's an odd kind of family, but, hey, what's normal?

"Amy?" he says, interrupting my thoughts. "I couldn't love you more if you were my own daughter, you know that, right?"

"I love you too, Dave," I say. It's the first time I've said it, but it feels right.

Dave smiles happily.

"Love oo, Dada," Alex pipes up, lifting his head from his coloring.

Dave and I laugh.

"And I love you, buddy," Dave tells him, and then right there, in the middle of the restaurant, he breaks into one of his Dinoduck songs: *I love you, I really do. Loving you makes me so happy too. Me so happy too, oh, me so happy too. . . .*"

I'm mortified. I stare down at the table, avoiding eye contact with anyone and willing myself to disappear.

It's a sweet song, though, and very catchy, and when Dave is finished, lots of people in the restaurant start to clap. I lift my head. OK, some are also giving him very strange looks, but he doesn't seem to care.

"Is that a new song?" I ask Dave when the clapping has stopped and my cheeks have finally stopped glowing with embarrassment.

"Yep. Do you like it? I'm *this* close to making Dinoduck a success, Amy." He pinches thumb and index finger together. "So close I can taste it. I just need to ace my meeting with Rolf Grant —"

"Rolf Grant? *The* Rolf Grant?" Even I've heard of Rolf Grant. He's the Irish music mogul who discovered Coast, the hugely popular Irish boy band.

"Yep," he says proudly. "He's listened to my CD, and he's agreed to see me. I'm just waiting to hear back from his people. It should be any day now. He's based in London and LA, but he's over in Dublin in a few weeks."

"That's mega-exciting, Dave," I say. I can't wait to tell Mills. She's mad about Billy, Coast's lead singer. If Rolf Grant is Dave's manager, maybe I can wangle her an up-close-and-personal with Billy.

"Does Mum know?" I ask him.

"No, I didn't want to give her false hopes. She

has enough on her mind with the wedding and everything. Other managers were interested at first, but they've all turned me down. One of them thought I was too old for the children's entertainment market. Old? I'm only thirty-two."

"That's ancient," I quip. "But don't worry, the meeting can be our big yellow Dinoduck secret."

"Thanks, Amy. And thanks for coming with me this morning too. It was fun. We should hang out together more often."

"Sure," I say, and I mean it. I'm lucky — it's pretty cool having two dads to spend time with, even if they are both a bit bonkers.

When we get home, Mum calls down the stairs. "Is that you, Dave?"

"No, it's me, Mum. Dave's getting Alex out of the car."

"Oh, good. Come on up quickly, Amy. I have something exciting to show you, and I don't want Dave to see it. I'll be in my room."

Curious, I run up the stairs and walk through the doorway to her bedroom.

"Ta-da!" Mum says, doing jazz hands. "What do you think?"

She's wearing an icy-white off-the-shoulder wedding dress. It has a curvy sweetheart silk bodice and a full, net-covered skirt dotted with silver sequins. It's nice and everything, it's just not really Mum.

"I got it for a song at the thrift shop. Eighty euros, can you believe it? What a bargain." She does a twirl, the skirt puffing out around her. "You're very quiet, Amy. What do you think?"

"It's lovely," I say, trying to sound enthusiastic.

"I know it's not the perfect dress, pet, but the dress isn't all that important."

Is she kidding? Even I know that choosing your wedding dress is a serious business.

"I'm marrying Dave, that's the important bit," she adds.

I'm still not persuaded. Yes, I know that ultimately marrying the right guy is the most important thing, but it's Mum's special day and she deserves to feel like a princess.

I really need to talk to Clover.

# ♥ Chapter 14

I'm in Clover's car a week later, driving toward Dundrum Shopping Centre to meet Lia, the girl who wrote to us asking for fashion tips. We're taking her shopping. Clover's calling it our "retail mercy mission." And Saffy managed to wangle a mega-shopping voucher from Dundrum to cover it.

"Did you get a chance to talk to Mum about the whole wedding dress thing?" I ask Clover as we pull away from the house.

"Yes. And she's firmly set on wearing the thrift shop bargain. She's determined not to spend any more money on the wedding. But let's not worry about that today. Sorry I've been incommunicado for a bit. Anything new with you?"

I tell her all about Seth's text and our phone call, and also what Dave said about Seth changing his mind about the breakup if I give him some time.

Clover thinks about this for a moment and then asks, "How were things in school this last week? With Seth, I mean."

"OK. We talked a little bit. Mainly about Polly and how she's doing. And about classics homework. Nothing major. But he was pretty nice to me."

"It's hard to know with boys, Beanie, but it sounds like Dave could be right. Hang in there. I think you just have to play the waiting game for now."

I sigh deeply. "I know, but it's so hard."

"My heart goes out to you, Glum Bean, really it does. But maybe today's shopping spree will help take your mind off things. There's nothing like spending someone else's moolah to put a smile on a girl's face."

When we get to Café Rua, a sweet little redbrick tearoom near Harvey Nichols, where Lia has arranged to meet us, the door is shut. There's a sign on it that reads, SORRY, CLOSED FOR A PRIVATE FUNCTION.

Clover looks puzzled. "Lia said Café Rua, right?"

I try the door, but it's definitely locked. I try to

peer in through the window, but the blinds are down. Just then the door swings open, and standing there, wearing a long white-blond wig, is Eloise Oliphant. What is she doing here? And what's with the wig? Last autumn Clover and I helped Eloise overcome her fear of boys by inviting her to meet Alex, Seth, Dave, and Gramps, and Felix from the Golden Lions.

"Surprise!" Eloise says, breaking into a huge grin, her brown eyes twinkling. "In case you're wondering, there is no Lia. That was just a ruse to get you here today. Come on inside. The other girls are dying to meet you."

"Beanie?" Clover whispers to me. "Are you in on this? What's going on?"

"No idea, boss. Honest."

Inside, the place is packed with girls my age, all wearing exactly the same blond wig as Eloise. Most of them are also wearing sparkly tights, shorts, and biker boots, but a handful are dressed in black skinny jeans and stripy tops. The girls are staring at Clover like she's a movie star and whispering and giggling among themselves.

"Look!" I tell Clover excitedly. "They're dressed up as you! What is this, Eloise? Some sort of strange Clover Wildgust cult meeting?"

Eloise laughs. "I'll let Alanna tell you; it was her idea. She's been planning it for weeks with your editor's help. Alanna!"

A tall girl wiggles her way through the bodies and then claps her hands together to get everyone's attention. I recognize her from a video clip I watched last spring. She was modeling in a *Goss* magazine teen fashion show, sashaying up and down a catwalk in a swishy red dress. It was one of the things Clover set up for her after she had been the victim of horrible cyber-bullying. We wanted to fix things for her by giving her a starry, über-cool online presence that no one could tease her about ever again. From the way Clover is staring at Alanna, it's clear that she's recognized her too. And then the penny drops: every girl in this room is someone that Clover has helped in the agony-aunt pages of the *Goss*. Clover is still looking confused, though. I don't think she's figured it out yet.

Alanna claps her hands again. "Girls," she says to the room, "as you've probably guessed by now, this is Clover Wildgust from the *Goss* magazine, and her niece and co-problem-solver, Amy."

At that, the girls all start cheering and whooping and throwing their arms in the air like they're at a field hockey game.

Alanna turns to me and Clover. "And as you've probably guessed by now, we're just some of the girls you've helped over the past year. And we're all here today to say a great big thank-you. You guys have turned our lives around. You might not know our faces but you may remember our names. And some of the gang would like to say a few words. Dominique, would you like to go first? I know Clover and Amy's help meant a lot to you."

"Sure." A petite girl breaks away from the crowd. Under the wig, which looks huge on her head, she has beautiful coffee-colored skin, like Brains's, long, sweeping dark eyelashes, and striking hazel eyes.

"I wrote to you last December about my brother, Happo," she says, her voice surprisingly big for such a small girl. "I have to tell you all what these two did for me — it was amazing. Happo was taking this stuff called creatine. He's into rugby, and it's supposed to bulk you up. Anyway, he has a heart condition and I was worried — I thought it might hurt him, you know. So I wrote to the girls, and they set up a fake drugs test for Happo's team. It was a brilliant idea. It scared the living daylights out of them." She gives a laugh. "And from that day on, none of the guys have touched creatine or steroids or anything like that. It was a miracle. Clover and Amy may have saved

Happo's life. I'm so grateful—" She breaks off as she brushes tears out of her eyes. "Sorry," she says to us. "It's just you don't even know me, and you cared enough to help. It really is something."

"We love helping people," Clover says. "Don't we, Beanie—sorry, Amy?"

I smile at her. "Sure do. It was our pleasure to help, really."

"And you know that Dundrum voucher that Saffy gave you?" Alanna says. "It's for you both. From all of us."

"Seriously?" Clover gasps. "Girls, that's so sweet of you. You really didn't have to."

"We wanted to," Dominique says firmly.

"Boy, do you deserve it," says a girl with cornflower-blue eyes. "I'm Wendy, and you helped me take down a guy named Brett Stokes. Remember him? He told everyone I kissed like a washing machine. And you kissed him, Clover—actually kissed him—at a Sinister Frite Night and told everyone that he'd bitten you. His nickname is still Bram after that *Dracula* guy, and he hasn't spread false rumors about any girl since. You deserve a medal for what you did, Clover. You're incredible."

"And, Amy, I'm Carrie," one of the other girls says. She's even smaller than Dominique, with pale, creamy skin and a smattering of freckles on the bridge of her nose. "When my parents split up, you wrote me an amazing letter telling me about your own parents' separation. It made me feel less alone. Thank you."

One by one, each girl tells her own story, including Hannah, the swimmer who hated her body; Frizzy, who had three frenemies that didn't deserve her; and even Bethan, whose letter sparked my recent article about kissing. It's such a surreal but happy experience to listen to their stories and know that we really did make a difference to each and every one of them.

When they've finished talking, Clover says, "I don't know what to say, girls. I'm glad things have worked out for you all. I want to add my own thank you now. I couldn't have done any of this without Amy — she's my teen-problem-solver extraordinaire. She writes a lot of the letters, you know, and comes up with loads of great feature ideas too. She'll be taking over from me on the *Goss* any day now. Mark my words, she's got super smarts, that one. We're both so pleased we could help you. Meeting you all in person is amazing. How on earth did you find everyone, Alanna?"

"Through Saffy," Alanna explains. "She asked some clever techy guy who used to work for the magazine to find our original letters on the *Goss* mail server, and then she helped me contact everyone. And here we are."

Clover laughs. "That techy guy is my boyfriend, Brains! I knew he was hiding something."

"He's in the Golden Lions, isn't he?" Wendy pipes up. She's blushing. "I'm a huge fan. I can't believe he's your boyfriend. He's so cute. . . . He's always talking about you on their blog."

"Is he now?" Clover tries to look cross, but I can tell she's secretly thrilled.

"You have a rock-star boyfriend too?" Alanna says. "Clover, are you the coolest girl in the universe or what?"

"You're mighty, Clover," Dominique agrees.

She's right. Clover really is something.

Everyone cheers again, and then they all start chanting, "Clo-ver, Clo-ver, Clo-ver . . ."

♥ Chapter 15

Over the next two weeks nothing much changes between me and Seth. I talk to him at school and on the phone, but it's always about schoolwork and Polly. I never say what's really on my mind—how much I miss him, how I wish we could get back together. He never mentions anything about us either. It's all very friendly but reserved. I know everyone's told me to be patient and to give him time, but how much time exactly? Days? Weeks? Months? I'm not sure I can wait that long—not knowing what he's really thinking is doing my head in. And not being able to share with him how I truly feel is exhausting. I know he's having a tough time with Polly and everything, and I'm doing my best to be there for him—to listen to him when he needs to talk, to tell him that everything's going to be all right — but it's so hard. I'm not sure I can go on like this for much longer. Being close to him but not *with* him is agony.

On Friday in art class, Mr. Olen pairs everyone up to draw each other's faces. "Amy and Seth, I guess you'll want to gaze at each other, as usual, so you'd better team up together."

"Sir! That's unfair," I say instantly, my cheeks burning. Mr. Olen clearly hasn't noticed that Seth and I no longer even sit together. Besides, we were never a lovey-dovey couple! We're not Mills and Bailey!

"Just get on with it, please," he says. "I want you to take it in turns to draw each other. Study your partner's face, especially their eyes, and try to re-create the emotion you see there in your sketch. Find the essence of that person and translate it to paper."

"Do you want to go first, Amy?" Seth asks, after moving to my table.

"No, you can. I'll just sit here and try not to laugh."

"OK." Seth picks up his pencil and starts to sketch the outline of my face using quick, light pencil marks. His gaze meets mine every time he looks up and he studies my eyes carefully, his own giving nothing away. He's concentrating hard.

I try to tell Seth how I feel about him, through my eyes. *I'm confused,* I make them say. *And hurt and angry. What do you want? A friend or a girlfriend?* Suddenly Seth's eyes change; they're softer. He gives me a gentle smile. And I feel hope. Maybe he does still like me after all. . . .

"Seth," I say. It's difficult to get his name out.

He pulls his eyes away from me and stares down at the sheet of paper and concentrates on his sketch again, his hand moving expertly over the page.

I try to see what he's doing, but his other arm is curved around the paper, blocking my view. I watch him for a few more minutes. When he finally moves his arm, I gasp. His picture is extraordinary. He's caught me perfectly: my oval face, the wispy bits of my hair tucked behind my ears, the downward curve of my sad mouth. But my eyes are the most captivating feature of all — huge swirling pools of emotion that swallow up the viewer. *Love me,* they say. *Please, love me.* Seth's version of me looks so needy and lost. I take a few deep breaths and will myself not to cry. Breaking down in art class would be so embarrassing.

"Change over if you haven't already," Mr. Olen says.

Seth now sits silently staring at me, offering himself to me to draw. I sketch his face on my sheet and mark in the curved lines where his eyes and his mouth will go, like Mr. Olen showed us during another class. I re-create Seth's mouth, with his full lips. Then I move upward, trying to capture his high, angular cheekbones, the smattering of sun freckles over his nose and cheeks; the way his hair flops over his face. And finally, his eyes.

As I study them, taking in every fleck of each sky-blue iris, noticing again that the right one has a curved navy-blue fleck in it, the shape of a tiny dolphin, my heart is racing. *Come back to me, Seth,* I will him with my own eyes.

He stares at me for a long moment and then looks away. He whispers, "Amy, stop looking at me like that. We're just friends, OK?"

And there it is — as simple as that. Mills was wrong. Dave was wrong. Clover was wrong. Seth doesn't want me back — ever. I realize that I can't be "just friends" with him, even to help him through all the stuff with Polly. I can't! I still love him, and it's too much to ask. He's not being fair.

My eyes are welling up, so I run from the room, muttering, "Toilet, sir," as I pass Mr. Olen.

Once I'm out of sight of the classroom, I collapse on the steps up to the main school building and finally allow the tears to flow. I believed Mills and Dave and Clover. I thought that once everything with Polly had settled down, Seth would come back to me — would love me again. But clearly I was delusional.

I'm crying so much now I can barely breathe. Oh, Seth.

♥ Chapter 16

After I told Mills what had happened in art class, she invited me to her house after school so we could talk about it properly. She really is a great friend. We're in her room now, and she's trying to make me feel better about Seth and my broken heart, but it's not doing much good.

"You need to take some time to get over him," she says gently. "There'll be other boys. Look at Ed. I was mad about him, but it just wasn't meant to be." Ed was Mills's first boyfriend. She met him in Miami last summer, and he broke up with her by e-mail. Ouch!

"Not like Seth, there won't," I say. "And I don't want anyone else, I just want *him*. I can't bear it, Mills. Why does it have to hurt so much?"

"Oh, Ames, if I could fix it for you, I would." She gives me a hug. "I hate seeing you so upset. Do you want to watch a movie or something? It might help take your mind off things."

"OK, but nothing smoochy. I couldn't bear it. How about a horror movie?"

"You hate horror movies!"

"I know, but you love them. I'll shut my eyes during the gory bits."

So we watch *The Others*, one of Mills's sister Claire's old DVDs. It's a creepy film about ghosts and hauntings, and according to Mills, it's a horror "classic." Thankfully it's not too gory, but I still hate every dark and dismal minute of it. However, it does match my mood perfectly.

Clover rings me at nine o'clock on Saturday morning, waking me up.

"Clover?" I ask her groggily. I didn't get back from Mills's until late. "Is anything wrong?"

"Nothing at all, Beanie. In fact, things are most definitely *right*. But I need your help. Is Dave there this morning?"

"I think so. I don't think he's working this weekend."

"Good. Tell him we need Sylvie this morning on

157 ♥

urgent wedding-dress business. Get your mum up and dressed and looking respectable, and I'll be over to collect you both in half an hour. If she asks, don't mention wedding dresses. Make something up."

"Wedding dresses? What's going on, Clover?" But she's gone. Great — I so obviously need even more drama in my life!

At half past nine on the dot Clover bustles us into her Mini Cooper. "Chop-chop, don't want to be late," she says, practically pushing me into the backseat.

"Late for *what* exactly, Clover?" Mum asks. "I'm not in the mood for Dundrum. Promise me we're not going to be trailing around shops. Amy said it's something to do with the wedding favors, but I thought we'd decided against those."

Clover gives me a "Nice one, Beanie" wink. "All will be revealed soon, Sylvie," she says, "but there will be no shopping, I promise. Right, I'm not saying another word about it until we get there, understand? Life's dreadfully boring without the odd surprise to perk it up."

"I hate surprises," Mum moans. "Can't you just tell us now, Clover?"

"That would be a negative. Now, Golden Lions, anyone? Brains gave me a CD of their new songs."

"Any of them about you, Clover?" I ask. Brains has already written a song about Clover. He couldn't make "Clover" fit into his song lyrics, though, so he called her Caroline instead. It was a big hit and got loads of airplay.

"And that would be an affirmative." She grins and switches on the car stereo. A strong drumbeat fills the car, followed by a jangle of guitars and then Brains's strong, husky voice rings out: *"Baby, won't you be mine? Be my one and only Valentine? One and one make two. I wanna marry you, marry you, marry you."*

Mum starts to giggle nervously. "Gosh, sis, is he serious? Aren't you both a bit young for that kind of commitment?"

"No kidding. Marriage is for olds. Like you and Dave."

"Do you mind? I'm in my prime. Hey, that almost rhymes — maybe I could write a song too. Like Dave and Brains. How hard can it be?"

"One songwriter in the family is enough, Mum," I say. I'm about to ask her if Dave has heard about his Dinoduck meeting with Rolf Grant, but I remember just in time that it's a secret.

"Two, if I marry Brains," Clover says, then shrugs. "In the future, I mean. When I'm all grown up."

I grin. "Like that's ever going to happen, Clover. Seriously!"

"Touché, Beanie," she says. And then we all start to laugh.

After parking just off Kildare Street, Clover heads toward Dawson Street. Mum and I scurry behind her, like rats after the Pied Piper.

Mum is groaning. "I thought you promised no shopping. It's Saturday, Grafton Street will be heaving." Grafton Street is one of the biggest shopping streets in Ireland, home to Brown Thomas department store and many other cool shops.

"I did," Clover says. "And a promise is a promise. We're here." She points at a gold plaque beside a large red door. It reads THE GOSS.

"Your office? Why are we at your office, Clover?" Mum looks baffled.

Clover just smiles. "Patience, Grasshopper."

Mum rolls her eyes. "Clover! Tell me you did not drag me the whole way into town so you could pick something up from work?"

"As if, Sylvie. But we *are* going inside."

"Really?" I ask excitedly. I've always wanted to visit Clover's office.

"Abso-doodle-lutely, Beanie." Clover takes out

what looks like a credit card and swipes it through a discreet brown box attached to the side of the door. There's a buzz and the door clicks open.

"This had better be worth it, Clover," Mum says. "If it is some sort of wild goose chase, I'll kill you."

I thought the *Goss* office would be all high-tech and modern, with glossy white walls and chrome, leather seating, and maybe even an acrylic desk, but the hallway is paneled with squares of dark wood, and there's a musty smell. It's like walking into an old church.

"Not quite what you were expecting, is it, Bean Machine?" Clover says.

"Not exactly."

"It's an old building. But wait till you get upstairs. It's got a bit more pizzazz."

Clover starts walking up the wooden staircase, and once again, we follow her. We go up one flight and then through a door. We enter a small reception area that's gleaming white, with dozens of framed magazine covers hanging on the walls, picked out by a row of tiny spotlights. There's a white-and-chrome desk, with a matching leather-and-chrome swivel chair. OK, this is more like it!

"That you, Clover?" A petite woman emerges from the door to the left of the reception area and walks

161 ♥

toward us. She's wearing a black silk jumpsuit teamed with pink-and-purple leather high-tops. Her hair is orange and cut into a cute pixie crop. Enormous blue plastic geek glasses frame her hazel eyes.

"Hey, Clover," she says, then kisses her warmly on both cheeks. "And this must be your niece." She smiles at me, her eyes sparkling. "I'm Saffy. The editor around these parts. Saffron Cleaver, to be precise. And I do like to be precise. Not enough precision in this world, if you ask me. Clover never stops talking about you, Amy. Or should I call you Beanie?"

"Amy's good," I say. "I'm Beanie only to Clover."

"Excellent, Amy it is. And finally the wedding belle, am I correct?" Saffy turns to Mum. "It's a pleasure to meet you."

"That's right. I'm Sylvie," Mum says, shaking Saffy's hand. "Nice to meet you too." Mum looks completely bewildered. She's clearly wondering what on earth we are doing here. I'm curious too. I have a strong suspicion that Clover and Saffy have something rather special up their fashionable sleeves.

"As you know, Clover has been working with us for some time now," Saffy continues. "She's become an invaluable member of the team and has saved my bacon on a number of occasions. She even stepped in for my friend Hettie at the wedding fair. As a special thank-you and to celebrate her general wonderfulness, I told Clover she could have her pick of the fashion cupboard. Anything she likes — a Mulberry bag, a Prada dress, a Gucci jacket. . . . She deserves it. Hettie was there at the time and joked that she could have her pick of the *Irish Bride*'s wardrobe too. So guess what Clover chose?"

I smile to myself. I think I see where this is going.

"Sylvie," Clover says. "I know you've got your thrift store dress and that for you the most important thing is marrying Dave, but please let me do this for you. You've done so much for me over the years, and this is my way of saying thank you. The *Irish Bride* cupboard is full of beautiful wedding dresses, and Hettie said I could take my pick. Saffy's even offered to help find the perfect one for you. I really want you to look stunning on your wedding day. Please say yes."

"Are you sure, Clover?" Mum asks. "A Mulberry handbag does sound pretty tempting."

"Positive. Seeing you sparkle on your wedding day is worth hundreds of handbags, Sylvie."

Mum smiles. "Then I guess it's a yes."

"Excellent," Saffy says. "Now, we'd better get moving, I have a lunch date at one. Hettie's office is crammed with dresses, as they've just shot the wedding spreads for their May edition. This could take some time."

Saffy's right. Even though Hettie's office is large, it is so stuffed with wedding dresses, we can barely move. Gowns hang from rails, others lie over the backs of chairs in white zipped-up bags, and some are simply piled on top of her desk. And it's not just frocks; the room is also full of shoes, hats, veils, bags, and jewelry.

"Mamma mia," Clover says. "Wedding dresses a-go-go."

Mum is starting to look rather scared. "So many dresses," she whispers.

Saffy immediately takes control, which is something she seems rather good at. "Don't panic. Hettie said that it may look like chaos, but there is method to the madness. The dresses are broken down into shapes and styles. She also said to help yourself to accessories if you need them."

Mum, who has been staring at a pair of pale-pink sandals with diamanté butterflies on the toes, gasps. "Really?" Her eyes are still glued to the shoes. "Are you sure, Saffy?"

"Go for it, babes," Saffy says.

Mum slips her feet into the shoes and sighs dreamily. "They're heavenly."

Saffy smiles. "I'm starting to feel a bit like the fairy godmother in *Cinderella*. A younger, hip version, natch! Now let's get down to business, babes. Clover and Amy, I could murder an Americano. Would you be angels and fetch one? And what about you, Sylvie?"

"Cappuccino, please. But don't we need their opinion?"

"No," Saffy says firmly. "Your opinion is the only one that matters, Sylvie, and having them around would just complicate things. You're in safe hands with me. I've dressed so many women, it would boggle your mind. I know what I'm doing."

"She really does," Clover assures Mum. "Trust me. She's dressed two Irish presidents and loads of big pop stars."

Mum still looks a little uncertain, but she says, "OK then, do your worst, Saffy."


Clover and I are both standing in front of Mum. And I'm embarrassed to admit that we're both crying our eyes out.

"Oh, sis, you look so . . . so . . ." For once in her life, Clover is lost for words. She waves her hand in front of her face, overcome.

"Beautiful," I finish for her. "And Cassandra was wrong — lace is so pretty on you. But it's nothing like the tacky shiny-looking lace her dresses were made from."

"Stunning, isn't it?" Saffy says, running her fingers over the delicate material. "So delicate, like a spider's web."

Mum's wearing a simple soft white lace gown with a V-neck and a flattering full skirt that is gently fitted at the waist and then skims her hips and rests just off the ground. Peeping out from underneath, like shy twins, are the pink shoes with the butterflies on the toes. Mum's hair is gathered up into a loose chignon. She's also wearing delicate crystal drop earrings that look like flower petals, and a matching crystal bracelet.

But the best thing of all is the beam on Mum's face. She looks radiant.

"We tried lots of different styles," Saffy says, "but I think this one captures Sylvie's essence the best — fun, artsy, a free spirit."

"Yes!" Mum says. "Exactly."

A free spirit? Does Mum really see herself that way? Clover winks and leans towards me. "Your mum was wild in her day," she says in a low voice. "Before she met Art and went all boring. Dave's perked her up a bit, mind. Maybe she'll be one of those mad old women who dyes her hair purple. Wild by name, wild by nature."

"What are you two whispering about?" Mum asks.

"Nothing," Clover says. "Just saying how lovely you look, sis. Dave will be blown away. Saffy, you're a genius."

"I am rather talented, aren't I?" Saffy says with a grin. "Now, Sylvie tells me that you're one of her bridesmaids, Amy. Care to write about your experience for the magazine? A guide to how to be the perfect bridesmaid would go down really well with our readers. I did adore that guide to kissing —"

"That Clover wrote," I cut in.

Saffy smiles knowingly at me. "Yes, of course. I'm very glad to have finally met you, Amy Green. Very glad indeed." She looks like she's about to say something else, but then she catches Clover's eye. Something in Clover's expression makes her stop. I wonder what that's all about. Before I get a chance to ask, Saffy is looking at her watch. "Now I must dash. Clover, be an angel and lock up for me. I promised Vivienne that I wouldn't be late. She does love lunch at the Merrion when she visits Dublin. Toodles, everyone."

"Vivienne Westwood?" Clover asks, her eyes wide, but Saffy has already gone.

"So that's Saffy?" I say. "All I can say is wow!"

Clover smiles. "Is there anyone cooler?"

"Yes," I say. "You, Clover. Look at Mum's face."

Mum is still staring at herself in the mirror and twirling this way and that. She's beaming. Clover gives me a hug. "Our girl is getting married. And she looks so happy. Bless her little cotton socks."

And then, marshmallows that we are, we both start crying again.

# ♥ Chapter 17

It's impossible to concentrate in school when Mum and Dave's wedding is only eight days away. It's on Tuesday, April 30, my birthday — although everyone's so caught up in the wedding plans, I think they've forgotten that I'm about to turn fourteen.

On Sunday night I begged Mum to give me the week off school. "Clover needs me, Mum," I told her. "I'm her assistant wedding planner, remember?"

But she wasn't falling for it. "My ultra-organized sister has everything under control," she said firmly. "I'm sure she can manage without your help. You have summer exams soon, Amy. You can't be skipping a whole week of school."

I rolled my eyes at her. What is it with parentals and exams? Besides, they're weeks away. If I study now,

I'll have forgotten everything by then. Cramming the night before is far more sensible, if you ask me.

Monday and Tuesday crawl by, but at least today, Wednesday, is a half day, so I get to help with the wedding preparations. After school, Mills and I are going to help Clover make the place names for the tables. This may sound easy, but it so isn't. Clover has decided that the guys' names will be painted on — get this — tiny guitars made out of modeling clay, 'cause Dave is such a music-head, and the girls' names will be painted on tiny books, to represent Mum's writing career. And guess who has to make forty-three mini-guitars and forty-one tiny books out of quick-drying modeling clay! Yep, that would be Clover's little elves, me and Mills!

I'm walking toward the DART station to catch the train home with Mills, ready to slave over hot modeling clay (or cold and squishy clay probably), when I get the strange feeling that someone is following us. I spin around.

I'm surprised to see Annabelle Hamilton walking just behind us, alone. "Why are you following us, Annabelle?" I ask her. "And don't say you're getting the train. I know you usually get a lift."

Annabelle goes pink. "I wanted to say something to Mills."

"About the All Saints?" Mills asks. "Has the cup arrived? Is that it?" The All Saints won a silver medal and the cup for Best Newcomers at the National Cheerleading Championships, and Mills is thrilled. The cup is away being engraved, and when it arrives back, it will be displayed in the school's sports cabinet. Mills can't wait to see it.

Since Annabelle's fall in front of Mindy, she's been a bit nicer to Mills. And now that Nora-May is back in the squad, Mills loves cheer practice. "Kind of," Annabelle says to Mills now. "I never said thank you for catching me that day when Mindy came to training. I could have sprained my ankle, like Nora-May." She hesitates. "You're a good backstop — better than me. But if you ever tell anyone that I said that, Mills, I'll deny it and make your life miserable, got it?"

"Is this some sort of trick?" Mills says, looking around as if expecting the other D4s to jump out at us. "Are you videoing this?"

"No." Annabelle sighs. "Why are you being, like, all suspicious and stuff? I've said thanks, Mills, all right? Let's just call a truce. No need to make a big deal out of it. And I guess I'm sorry about Seth,

Amy, even though he's, like, a complete Emo. Being dumped sucks." She gulps. "Not that I'd know 'cause I totally dumped Hugo. Right, I'm off. I have, like, better places to be."

Mills and I stand staring at her disappearing back.

"Did that actually happen?" I say. "Did Annabelle just thank you? And say she was sorry about Seth?"

"Yep. In her own way, I think she did. Weird, huh?"

"Very weird. But I guess people really do change." I hook my arm through Mills's. "But if she's after you as a bestie, she'll have to fight me off first."

Mills laughs. "As if, Amy Green! It's me and you, forever."

Later that afternoon I'm still being a worker bee on the mini-book and mini-guitar production line when the doorbell rings. Mills has gone home for her dinner, so it's just me and Clover now. Mills is coming back over at seven, after eating and doing her homework. It's too early for her yet, though.

"I'll get it," I say. I swing the front door open. It's Dad, clutching a newspaper in his hand.

"What's up, Daddy-o?" I ask him.

"Yuck!" he says, staring at the sticky gray clay all over my hands. "What's that disgusting goo, Amy?"

Oops, it's all over the door latch too. I must remember to clean it off before Mum gets home. She's over at Gramps's house with Alex and Evie.

"Modeling clay."

"School project?"

"Not exactly. Wedding business." The customized place names are supposed to be a secret. "All will be revealed on the big day."

Dad's face drops. "That's why I'm here actually. Has Clover seen this?" He opens the *Evening Chronicle* and stabs at one of the inside pages with his finger.

I read the headline: DALKEY ISLAND LODGE GOES BUST. Dalkey Island Lodge is where Mum and Dave's wedding reception is being held. I instantly go cold, like someone's just injected my veins with ice.

"Are you OK, Amy?" I hear Dad's voice, but it sounds funny, like he's underwater. I nod but I still can't seem to get any words out.

"Have you talked to Clover today?" Dad asks me.

I nod again and point toward the kitchen, where Clover is still up to her elbows in modeling clay. "She's here."

"Good, I'd better tell her the bad news." He comes inside and closes the front door behind him. "You'd better sit down, Amy. You look very pale. I'm sorry, I shouldn't have sprung it on you like that."

"Sprung what on her?" Clover asks, appearing at the kitchen doorway.

"Clover, has anyone from Dalkey Island Lodge been in touch with you today?" Dad asks urgently, without even saying hello.

"No, everything's all arranged. I went over the final details with the banqueting manager last week. Why? What's wrong?"

"The hotel's just gone bust. Look." Dad passes her the newspaper.

She takes it off him with her sticky fingers and reads the headline and then the article, her eyes going wider and wider. Then she swears several times under her breath.

"I tried ringing the hotel as soon as I spotted the article," Dad says. "But they're not answering the phone. I rang someone I know in their bank, and she said that the owners owe a fortune to their suppliers. They've been declared bankrupt and have absconded to Portugal. The hotel's closed, Clover."

"But we'll get our money back, right? And they'll open up for the wedding. They have to."

Dad winces. "I'll be honest with you, it's not looking good."

"What? But Sylvie and Dave have paid a whopping deposit up front. They can't lose all that money, it's not fair. And if the place doesn't reopen, what then? We'll never find another venue on such short notice. We'll have to cancel the wedding, and Sylvie will be devastated. Why is this happening?" Clover puts her hands over her face and starts groaning.

Dad takes his mobile out of his suit jacket pocket. "I'll make some more phone calls, ring my lawyer to see what I can do about getting the deposit back. Wait there, girls."

He walks into the kitchen and closes the door behind him. He's going to see all the books and guitars, but right now that's the least of our worries.

"This is so not good, Beanie," Clover says, flopping down on the bottom stair, her legs sticking out in front of her. She blows out all her breath. "I knew it was all going too smoothly. I'm so stupid. I bet a proper wedding planner would have a backup venue. Sylvie's wedding is not going to happen and it's all my fault."

"It's not your fault, Clover, honestly. No one could've predicted something like this. And I'm sure Dad will be able to sort something out and get the money back. If the hotel isn't going to work out, we'll find another one. It'll be fine. You're super-fab at solving things, Clover, you'll think of something."

"You're very sweet, but the wedding's on Tuesday.

In less than a week. Oh, Beans, what am I going to do?"

"We," I remind her. "We're in this together, Clover." I squeeze in beside her on the stairs.

She rests her head on my shoulder. "Thanks. We've worked so hard on this wedding. I'll be devastated if it all goes wrong."

Dad comes out of the kitchen, his mobile still in his hand. "It's not looking good, girls," he says. "I'm so sorry. My lawyer will do her best, but apparently the hotel hasn't paid any of its insurance premiums this year. She thinks it's unlikely that you'll get anything back."

"No!" Clover says. "That's so unfair."

"Believe me, I agree. Now we have to come up with another plan for Tuesday."

"Is there any point, Art?" Clover says, sounding defeated. "It's probably too late to find anywhere on such short notice. And if the deposit really is gone, then we don't have enough money anyway. It's hopeless."

"But we have some money, right?" I ask her.

Clover sighs. "Yes, but only enough to cover a wedding breakfast at McDonald's, if we're lucky. It's a disaster. The hotel was organizing loads of other stuff too, like the flowers and the food. Even Sylvie's hair and makeup was booked at the hotel's salon as part of the deal. It really is a disaster of *Titanic* proportions."

Dad and I look at each other, but there's nothing more to say. Clover's right, the hotel going bust really is an epic disaster.

♥ Chapter 18

I call Mills to explain.

"I don't think we're going to be needing those place names after all," I tell her. "So you may as well stay at home."

"Why? What's happened?"

"We may have to cancel the wedding."

"What? Cancel it? Are you serious?"

I explain about the hotel going bust. "It's a catastrophe. It's not just the venue and the food. The hotel had arranged loads of extra things — even the flowers and Mum's hair."

"Can't you find somewhere else?" she asks.

"Clover and Dad are in the living room, ringing every hotel in Dublin, but it's not looking good.

Look, I'd better go. I have to ring the suit place and see if we can cancel the rental. I'll ring you later, OK?"

"I'm so sorry, Amy. Let me know if I can do anything."

"Thanks."

Next I ring Stan at Good Grooming and tell him the news.

"Ach, Amy, that's awful," he says. "Not the first time a venue's gone bust like this, I'm afraid." He pauses for a moment. "I'd really like to help you out if I can. You seem like nice folks, and Brains really saved my bacon that day at the wedding fair. Plus, your aunt Clover has arranged for my shop to be featured in *Irish Bride*. Now, think about this before you say anything, but I may have a venue solution for you. What about a tent? If you have somewhere to put it, I'll find one for you. I know all the wedding rental companies. They can also provide chairs and tables and a stage for your band. It's worth considering. All you'd need then is someone to do the food. I'll keep those suits on hold until I hear from you."

"Thanks, Stan. I'll talk to Clover and Dad and ring you straight back."

I put down the phone and rush into the living room.

"Stan's suggested a tent," I say. "He said he could

179 ♥

find one for us, and the tent company would also provide tables and chairs. Would Gramps's garden be large enough for a tent?"

"Who's Stan?" Dad asks.

"The wedding suit guy," Clover says. "He's a sweetheart. What do you think, Art? The lawn beside the house is pretty big."

Dad nods. "I think you're right. But we'd still need a caterer."

"And a florist. And a makeup artist. And a hairdresser," I remind him.

Just then the doorbell rings. Clover jumps up to get it. She comes back into the room with Mills's mum, Sue, behind her.

"Mills told me about the hotel," Sue says. "What a catastrophe, girls." She gives me a big hug. She's lovely that way. "My heart goes out to you all," she continues. "Mills said the hotel was supposed to be providing the flowers. Now, I did a flower-arranging course last year. We covered bridal bouquets and corsages. I'm not professional or anything, but I know my way around a tea rose. If you find a new venue, I'd be delighted to get the flowers from the market for you and arrange them for the wedding. I love Sylvie to bits and I'd really like to do this for her. And Mills has offered to help me."

"Looks like we now have a venue, seating, and flowers," Dad says. "So how about it, girls? Do we go for it? Get this wedding on the road? There must be someone out there who could do the food. We can start ringing all the catering companies tomorrow. And I'll happily order the drinks and the glasses."

"And I can do Sylvie's hair and makeup if we can't find anyone else," Clover says. "So I'm in. Amy?"

"Yes!" I say. "Let's do it. I guess the wedding's back on after all."

As soon as Sue's gone, Dad says, "Of course, we've forgotten something. Sylvie. Who's going to tell her and Dave about the change of plan? We'll also need to let the guests know. It might be best coming from you, Clover."

"Once we have everything in place, I'll talk to her," Clover promises. "She's the one who keeps saying that she wants a simple wedding. I'm sure she'll love the idea of a tent in Gramps's garden."

"Let's hope so," Dad says. "Or else we really are in trouble."

Later that evening, I get a phone call from Bailey. At least it's Bailey's number, but it's certainly not Bailey's voice.

"Amy, it's Finn, Bailey's dad. Remember me?"

"Of course I do." How could I forget Finn Hunter, the Irish Surfing Chef? He's always popping up on radio and TV chat shows.

"Mills has been talking to Bailey and I hear you need a chef for your mum's wedding on Tuesday. I'd like to offer my services. You've been a really good friend to Bailey, Amy. I'd like to repay the favor."

A celebrity chef cooking at Mum's wedding? Things are looking up. And Mum adores Finn Hunter — she still kisses the telly screen when he comes on. She's going to be over the moon! Maybe this wedding isn't going to be such a disaster after all.

I turn out to be right. Mum is thrilled that Finn is doing the catering. "Finn Hunter? At my wedding? Are you serious? I love Finn Hunter!" is the first thing she says when Clover breaks the news about the change in venue and everything over dinner the following evening. She and Dad spent the whole day getting the new wedding details sorted.

It looks like wedding Mark II is a-go-go!

♥ Chapter 19

When I wake up on Tuesday morning—Mum and Dave's wedding day—I jump out of bed, throw back my curtains, and nearly cry with relief. Clover and I have been checking out weather apps obsessively all week, terrified that Mum's big day would be spoiled by buckets of rain. Or even hailstones or snow—the weather has been so weird lately. But it's sunny, and there's not a cloud in the sky. Sun, in Ireland, in April—it's a miracle! I sigh with relief. It's a good omen—it just has to be. Plus, it's also my birthday. Another good omen.

"Happy birthday, Amy," I whisper to myself. We're celebrating next weekend on account of the wedding, and I can't help feeling a little down. It's not every day that you turn fourteen. Fourteen! It sounds so much older than thirteen. Like the difference between seventeen and full-on-adult eighteen, the biggest jump there is. Still, it's Mum's special day and I don't really mind waiting to celebrate my birthday. Well, only a bit.

I check my phone. Two "happy birthday" messages — from Dad and Mills. I'm glad they've remembered. Then I hear a scuffling sound and low, hushed voices outside my door, followed by Alex's frantic giggling. He's probably doing his hideous new naked dance, wiggling his bum, slapping it with his hand, and yelling "Yee-ha!" He saw the move in some music video on the telly and has been doing it ever since. He added the "Yee-ha!" bit all by himself, odd little troll that he is. The more we all tell him to stop, the more he keeps on doing it.

I put my mobile down, yank open the door, all ready to let him have it — and get the fright of my life when I find Alex, Mum, Clover, and Evie outside.

Clover yells, "Surprise!" and waves a huge silver helium balloon in my face. It has 14 TODAY printed on it in rainbow colors.

Mum's in her dressing gown with Evie in her arms and Alex at her feet. And, yes, as I suspected, Alex is naked. Evie, however, is wearing her fluffy pink sleep suit with the hood and the floppy ears. She looks all cute and cuddly, like a little pink bunny.

"Happy birthday, love," Mum says, smiling at me, then leans over to give me a kiss on the cheek. She smells just-out-of-the-shower fresh. Her hair's wet, in fact, and is hanging down her back in a sleek wave. She had it highlighted and trimmed last week and the ends are still sharp. There are dark circles under her eyes, though, and her face is a bit pinched and tense. I guess it is a big day for her, and she's probably been worrying all night about something going wrong.

Dave spent last night at his friend Russ's house — apparently it's bad luck for the groom to see the bride on the night before the wedding.

"Let's go downstairs and have some breakfast together before the day starts to get even more manic," Mum says, yawning. Which sets me off.

I yawn so deeply that my jaw cracks. "It's not even eight yet, Mum."

"I know, but it's a busy day. There's still a lot to do."

"All you have to worry about this morning is being beautified, Sylvie," Clover says firmly. "Gramps will be here any minute to take the kids off your hands. And my very able assistant and I have everything under control, don't we, Bean Machine?"

Clover checks her watch. "In fact, our fabulous hair and beauty professional will be here very soon." Saffy was coming along to the wedding anyway, but when Clover asked her to recommend a last-minute makeup artist who wouldn't cost the earth, Saffy offered to do it herself. She worked on the MAC counter in Brown Thomas department store during college and loves making people look their best.

"So let's eat, people. Chop-chop." Clover practically pushes me down the stairs.

I get another surprise when I walk into the kitchen. The breakfast table is beautifully set and decorated with table confetti: tiny baby-blue 14s wink up at me. Alex grabs a handful and throws them in my face. One of them nearly lands in my eye.

"'Appy birf-day, Mimi," he says, giggling away to himself.

"Thanks, Alex," I say, wiping away the confetti.

After popping Evie into her high chair, Mum wrestles a fresh diaper and Thomas the Tank Engine pajamas onto Alex. He's not happy and squeals and wiggles so much that she has to scold him several times. He loves being naked; he'd spend all day in the nip if Mum let him. When he's decent, she lifts him into his high chair and finally flops down on one of the kitchen chairs.

"If that child starts stripping during the ceremony, I'll have a nervous breakdown," she says. "Keep your eye on him, Amy, will you? And Alex, you have to keep your clothes on today, buddy, understand?"

Alex gives Mum one of his angelic smiles. With his blond curls and bright-blue eyes, he looks like a little cherub, but he's more like a tiny Tasmanian devil.

"I love oo, Mummy," he says.

She laughs and pats his head. "I know you do, you charmer, but none of your tricks at the wedding, got it?"

Alex nods and says, "OK, Mummy" with such a serious little face that we all start to laugh. He grins, lapping up all the attention.

"Take a pew, Beanie," Clover says, pointing at a chair with a pink helium BIRTHDAY GIRL balloon attached to the back of it. There's a pile of wrapped presents and envelopes on the table. I'm so pleased that I almost start to cry. I thought everyone would be too caught up in wedding fever to remember my birthday. Clover's eyes are twinkling, and I realize that she must be behind the extraspecial treatment. Mum and Dave always remember my birthday, but I've never had table confetti or balloons before.

"Go on," Clover says. "Open your presents."

"I think I'll wait until after breakfast," I say, trying to keep a straight face. Clover has no patience whatsoever when it comes to presents. She always tears into the wrapping paper, ripping it off like there's a bomb inside that will explode if she doesn't extract the present within three seconds flat.

"Beanie!" she groans.

"Only kidding." I pick up the first present in the pile, a large square one covered in red-and-gold Christmas paper.

"Sorry, I couldn't find any birthday paper in the house," Mum says sheepishly. "I did buy some, but Alex used it as a sword, and it unraveled and ended up all over the garden."

"That's OK," I say with a smile. I tear off the paper to reveal a white shoe box. I open the lid and peer inside. Brand-new Converse — black high-tops covered in shiny black sequins. Mum has also tucked a Benefit eye shadow compact into one shoe and an iTunes voucher into the other.

"Thanks, Mum." I beam at her, delighted. She has been known to buy me the oddest presents, like a cricket set (and I don't even play cricket — she said the point was that I could learn) and bed linen. I mean, come on, who wants bed linen for their birthday?

No, this is pretty much the best present Mum has ever given me. "Can I wear the Converse today?"

"I'm glad you like them, Amy, but I'm not sure they'd go with your bridesmaid's dress."

The second present is from Alex and Evie — a summer scarf in light-gray cotton with black butterflies printed all over it. Again, pretty cool. Dad has given me a card with money tucked inside as usual — 100 euros this time. Yeah! And, for once, Mum doesn't sniff and comment on it being a "cop-out present."

There's a gift card from Gramps and, surprisingly, a pretty photographic card with a beach scene on it from Pauline, Shelly's mum. We haven't always seen eye to eye, Pauline and I, so it's nice that she's remembered my fourteenth.

The last envelope, a plain white one, is much bigger than the others. My name is written on the outside in shiny pink letters. I look over at Clover.

She nods. "That's from me, Beanie. Part one of your present. I'll give you part two later."

I open the envelope. Inside is a single sheet of paper with "Look in the living room" written on it.

"Go on," Clover says. "It's waiting for you."

"I'm going, I'm going." I grin at her, then Clover and I march off to the living room. I hear Mum tell

Alex to stay put, that she'll only be a second, and then she joins us. There's a huge rectangular present, the size of a car windshield, resting against the sofa. It's covered in red paper dotted with white hearts. I make a careful rip in the paper and laugh as I realize what's inside: a montage of photographs of me and Clover printed on glossy canvas.

Me and Clover in the kitchen wearing swimming goggles, making funny faces for the camera (Clover always wears goggles while cutting up onions); me and Clover wearing Santa hats last Christmas; me and Clover swimming on Killiney beach with Granny before she died; me, Clover, and Mum at Mum's *Sex and the City* bachelorette party in our costumes. . . . It's amazing. It must have taken her ages to pull all the images together.

"I love it, Clover!" I say, grinning up at her.

"Coola boola," she says. "Now let's eat, I'm starving. You promised me scrambled eggs with posh smoked salmon, Sylvie. Not to mention Buck's Fizz. And a wee taste for Beanie too — bridesmaid's privilege."

"OK," Mum says, "but just a tiny sip. I've got enough to be worrying about today without a tipsy teenager on my hands."

"I bet Dave and Russ aren't breaking out the

bubbly and the smoked salmon," Clover says. "Greasy fry-up for them, I'd say. Men!" She rolls her eyes. "No sense of occasion."

The phone rings as I'm sitting in the living room, our wedding-planning headquarters for the morning, checking our to-do list.

"Amy, can you hear me?" It's Dave. Ah, the groom himself.

"Hi, Dave. Just about, the line's very bad. Where are you?"

"In a lift at the Dublin Airport Hotel."

"What?"

"Look, it's a long story. I'm meeting . . ." The line goes all crackly.

"Say again?"

"I can't get through to Clover. Can you give her a message?"

"OK, sure. Go ahead."

"If I'm a little bit late for the service, don't panic. I'll definitely be there. I'm finally meeting Rolf Grant. His PA rang first thing this morning, said that he had a cancellation. I know it's terrible timing. . . ." I lose him again. "Once-in-a-lifetime chance, Amy, and I'm sure Sylvie . . ." The line goes dead.

I try ringing him back, but there's no answer.

Luckily Clover walks into the living room then, clicking her own phone off. "OK, Sue and Mills are in the tent. Sue's already dropped off Sylvie's bouquet. It's in the kitchen. You all right, Beanie? You look pale."

"I just had a call from Dave. He wanted to give you a message. He said he might be a bit late for the service. But he said not to worry — he'd definitely be there."

"Where is he exactly? He's supposed to go straight to the ceremony from Russ's house."

"Now, don't shoot the messenger, but he's at the Dublin Airport Hotel, meeting Rolf Grant."

"What? How could he? It's his wedding day. Is he crazy?"

"It wasn't planned, Clover. He's been trying to get a meeting for ages and Rolf had a cancellation today, apparently. Dave said it was a once-in-a-lifetime opportunity."

"So is marrying my sister!" Clover gives a strangled scream. "I could kill him. After we managed to salvage the wedding, he could ruin everything. We have the town hall for an hour only. If he's late, there will be no ceremony — it's as simple as that."

"He promised he'd make the wedding. And Dave always keeps his promises. He's a good guy, Clover. He's doing all this Dinoduck stuff for Mum too."

Clover sighs. "I know. It's just such horrible timing. And my nerves are shattered as it is."

"He'll be there," I assure her. But I hope I'm right. And I thought the sun this morning was a good omen. How wrong can you be?

# ♥ Chapter 20

"You're very quiet, you two," Mum says. We're all in an ultra-smart black limo — Mum, Clover, Monique, and me: the bride and her bridesmaids. We're on our way to the town hall for the wedding ceremony. If Dave turns up in time, that is!

"Just having a little time out," Clover says, giving Mum a big smile. "It's been a busy morning." She squeezes Mum's hand. "I know I've said it before, but you look beautiful, sis."

"Thanks," Mum says happily and then goes back to chatting to Monique about Monique's latest acting job.

My eyes meet Clover's and she gives me a gentle "It's going to be OK" smile. I nod back at her, but I'm so worried I can barely breathe. My iPhone is clutched in my sweaty palm. It's on silent, and every few seconds I swear I feel it vibrate against my skin, but when I look down, the screen is always dark, dead. *Come on, Dave. Contact me or Clover. Please.* We've tried ringing him and Russ dozens of times, but both their phones are going straight to messages.

I know Clover's just as frantic to hear from him as I am. She's just better at hiding her anxiety. Mum thinks I'm waiting for Seth to text me back, to confirm that he won't be at the wedding. He was invited before we broke up, and he still hasn't sent an RSVP, which is messing up our table plan. We don't know whether to set a place for him or not. I sent him a text this morning: PLEASE CONFIRM THAT YOU'RE NOT COMING TO THE WEDDING. AMY

There's no way he's going to turn up. Why would he? We're not together anymore, and he's made it quite clear that he has no interest in me other than being friends. I told Clover not to include him on the seating plan, but she has this crazy idea that he's going to appear at some stage today. She's still convinced that he loves me and has just been having a major emotional wobble because of Polly's illness. She's deranged! I let Mum think that it's Seth's text I'm waiting for, though. If she knew the truth, she'd freak out.

I look at Mum again, trying to keep my mind from thinking the worst — that Dave will be so late we'll have to cancel the whole wedding. It would be such a waste. Clover and I have put so much work into it, and Mum really does look beautiful, all thanks to Saffy. She's given Mum a lovely natural look: light foundation, a dusting of pink blusher on the apples of her cheeks, warm golden-brown eye shadow on her eyelids and a honey-colored lip stain on her lips, with a slick of gloss on top to make them shine. Her hair is swept back in a loose chignon and fastened with diamanté star clips. She's holding a simple round posy of the palest pink tea roses (they match her shoes perfectly), bound together with cream ribbon and tied off in a pretty bow. Sue did a brilliant job with the flowers. Mum is thrilled.

We've been blown away by how amazingly kind everyone has been since we heard about the hotel going bust. Even Seth's mum, Polly, is helping out, which makes it really weird that Seth hasn't replied to my text. Finn told Polly the news — they've become friends through the boys. Mills is convinced that they're secretly dating, but I think they just enjoy each other's company. Anyway, Polly rang me and offered to do the photography. It had been yet another thing that the hotel had arranged. Both Gramps and

Russ had offered to take some photos, but Polly is a professional, and I know Mum and Dave would love some nice images of the day to frame.

"Thanks, Polly, that would be brilliant," I told her.

"I'd be delighted to help," she said. "I miss you, Amy. Look, I shouldn't be saying this, and Seth will kill me, but I'm sorry about you guys breaking up. You were good together. He's been so down lately. He shouldn't be worrying about me, though — the new treatment's going well, and Dr. Shine is really pleased with my progress. I'm going to be fine. Anyway, my mouth is running away with me as usual. I just wanted to say that I'm sorry and I hope you're OK. I'll see you at the wedding. Let me know what time suits."

After the phone call, I sat very still with a big lump in my throat, thinking about what Polly had just said. If she was doing well, Seth had no reason to keep me at arm's length anymore. And if that was the case, he'd clearly just gone off me. Simple as that. Even though it was hard, I realized it was something that I'd just have to accept. I'd have to move on. At least I had plenty to think about — the wedding, for starters. Mum has been so stressed out about it. Looking after her has been a full-time job for me and Clover — and now Dave's gone missing! If he doesn't turn up, I think Mum will self-combust.

We arrive at the Dun Laoghaire town hall at ten to three. As Dave's family is Jewish and Mum is Church of Ireland, they decided to get married in a neutral setting, somewhere local that means something to both of them. They first met in Dun Laoghaire, when Dave was playing at a music festival in the People's Park.

The wedding ceremony starts in ten minutes, and wedding guests are piling into the building. I spot Dave's sister, Prue, carrying baby Bella in her arms. Ollie and Denis are following behind her, looking like kids from a Ralph Lauren ad in chinos and sky-blue shirts, with their hair neatly combed. Denis, who's ten, is holding Ollie's hand, and they look so cute.

Clover asks the driver to park down by the sea for a few minutes to wait for everyone to take their seats. Then she excuses herself and steps out of the limo to make a phone call, to Dave, I presume. I follow her.

"Any luck?" I ask, when she takes the phone away from her ear without leaving a message.

She shakes her head. "I'll try Dan. Maybe he or one of the ushers knows something we don't. Hi, Dan, it's Clover . . ."

That's a relief. At least he's answering his phone. Dan is Prue's husband and Dave's other best man — he's a really nice guy; dark-haired and smiley. "Any sign of Dave or Russ?" Clover asks him. There's a pause and then she sighs. "Roger that! We'll stay in a holding pattern." She clicks off her phone and frowns. "No sign of them, Beanie. I'm starting to get mega-, mega-anxious."

I check my watch. Five past three. Dave's now over half an hour late — he was supposed to be at the town hall at two thirty. This isn't looking good. I brush down the pink-chiffon ballerina-style skirt of my bridesmaid's dress nervously and adjust my lime-green cropped jacket. Clover's dress is mint-green, with a contrasting pink jacket, and Monique is wearing a full-length dark-green dress. They're not exactly traditional bridesmaids' dresses, but we all love them, Mum included, and that's the most important thing. A Parisian friend of Monique's designed them, and the trip to Paris to choose them was truly ooh-la-la!

The car door opens and Monique steps out. Saffy gave us all natural-looking makeup to match Mum's, but Monique insisted on her signature slash of poppy-red lipstick. She looks like the star she is.

"Any sign of Dave?" she whispers. Clover pulled her aside earlier and filled her in.

Clover shakes her head glumly.

"*Merde*," Monique says. "I think Sylvie's starting to get suspicious. I'll try to distract her."

As soon as Monique is back inside the car, Clover lets out an almighty moan. "*Siúcra*, Beanie, tell me this isn't happening."

The passenger window buzzes down and Mum's head appears. "Is everything all right, girls? What's the delay?" She looks from me to Clover and then gasps. "Something's wrong, isn't it? Oh, God, please no! No! Tell me he hasn't gotten cold feet." Her eyes start to well up.

"Mum, stop!" I say. "He's on the way, he just got stuck in traffic. Don't cry, you'll ruin your makeup."

"From Killiney?" Mum asks.

"He had to collect something in town," I improvise. "A special surprise for you. A wedding day present."

"But we said we weren't doing gifts for each other."

"You know guys," Clover says, waving her hand in the air. "Never listen."

Mum sighs, but thankfully her tears seem to have stopped. I think she's bought our story. "Men! So how much longer will he be?"

"Five minutes," I say at the exact same time that Clover says, "Ten minutes." Oops.

"I've known you both all your lives," Mum says, "and I can tell when you're lying. He's not coming, is he? And you're both trying to cover for him. I knew this was all too good to be true. Finally I find a nice man, someone kind and decent, and what happens? He can't commit." Her eyes go all blurry again. "I want to go home. I feel such a fool. How could he do this to me?"

"He's coming, Mum," I say urgently. "He promised. Just give him five more minutes. Please, Mum? I'm begging you. Don't give up on him." I swallow and blink hard, trying not to cry.

"Oh, Amy," Mum says. "I'm so sorry. I know this must be hard for you too. But we have to face facts. Dave's—"

My iPhone vibrates. It's a text—from Dave! ON THE WAY. TELL SYLVIE SORRY AND NOT TO PANIC AND THAT I LOVE HER. I HAVE GOOD NEWS, FANTASTIC NEWS. I'LL BE AT THE TOWN HALL IN TEN MINUTES. RUSS ALREADY HAS ONE TICKET FOR DRIVING IN THE BUS LANE, BUT HE SAYS IT'S WORTH IT. MEET YOU THERE! DAVE XXX

As I hand Mum the phone to read, I really do burst into tears—tears of relief.

"I'm sorry for doubting you, Amy," she says. "And for doubting Dave too. You must never, ever tell him what happened just now and what I said, girls. Do you understand? It has to be our secret. He'd be terribly upset. I was just really worried. . . ." She breaks off, sucking her breath in noisily and trying desperately not to cry again.

"You can trust us, Sylvie," Clover says. "Always."

"I know," Mum says. "That's why I love you both such a lot." And then she gets so emotional that we have to rush back into the limo for the tissues to save Saffy's beautiful makeup from running down her face.

♥ Chapter 21

We get Mum safely to the doors of the assembly room in the town hall, where the service is being held, without a major hitch. There is one minor hitch. However, it's nothing compared with all the drama-rama that's already happened this morning. We're halfway up the sweeping wooden staircase when there's a banging and a kerfuffle behind us.

"Don't turn around, Sylvie!" Russ shouts up the stairs.

Mum ignores him, spins around, and so do the rest of us. We stare down into the large tiled hallway. Russ scowls at her. "Please, Sylvie, it's important." He's holding a large black suit carrier over his arm and he looks surprisingly good in his morning suit and without his normal shaggy beard. In fact, he looks very handsome, and from the way Monique is checking him out, she clearly thinks so too.

"Is this something to do with my surprise?" Mum asks. "Is it in that suit carrier?"

Russ is clearly confused by Sylvie's question. He has no idea that we've told Mum about Dave being late because he was getting her a present. He recovers quickly, though. "Yes. Exactly. And no peeking, get it? Close your eyes, Sylvie, and keep them closed. OK?"

"Fine," Mum says huffily.

"I'll make sure she doesn't cheat," Monique says, batting her eyelashes at Russ. "And you look *magnifique*, Russ. So manly."

Russ blushes but looks delighted. "Thanks."

As soon as Mum's eyes are closed, he pushes open the front door, and Dave rushes inside in his fluffy yellow Dinoduck costume. He bounds up the stairs toward us. His face is bright red, and there are beads of sweat on his temples. I know for a fact that the Dinoduck costume is boiling to wear. I tried it on once and danced around the house for Alex and Evie, and I nearly passed out with the heat.

I have to press my hand against my mouth to stop myself from hooting with laugher, and Clover and Monique are just as bad.

"Hi, girls," Dave mouths at me and Clover as he

rushes past us, as quickly as he can in his costume. "Sorry."

We both roll our eyes and grin, and Clover hisses, "Hurry up" at him. I think we're all too relieved he's here to be annoyed with him.

"Say nothing," Russ whispers to me and Clover as he passes. He dashes through the doorway at the top of the stairs after Dave. "Give us three minutes."

Clover and I look at each other, then quickly follow them up the stairs. "Back in a second, Sylvie," Clover calls.

"We have to know," Clover says in a low voice when we catch up with Dave. "What did Rolf Grant say?"

"We're in," he says, his voice a bit ragged from all the running. "Rolf's going to take me on as long as I can persuade Russ and the other lads from the band to join me. Wants to change our name to Dino-Dad and the Evolutions. Says we could be the next big thing in kiddie rock."

"Seriously?" Clover asks.

Dave nods. "As soon as I give Rolf the go-ahead, he's going to start booking gigs at mother-and-toddler shows and stuff like that. He says we could be huge! Our money worries would be over and I'd get to play music for a living again."

"That's brilliant, Dave," I say, throwing my arms

around him. I kiss his hot, sweaty cheek and wince. "But now you'd better wash your face and get changed."

"Thanks, Amy. Tell Sylvie I can't wait to marry her." With that he rushes off toward the toilets with Russ.

"I genuinely thought I was going to have a heart attack if Dave didn't show," Clover says. "I've never been more relieved to see someone in my whole life."

"Me too." I blink away my tears. "Now let's pray that Alex doesn't strip during the vows."

I shed a few more tears walking up the aisle with Clover (although I'm not sure it's exactly an aisle, as we're in a town hall). Mum is in front, holding Gramps's arm tightly. She rests her head gently against his shoulder from time to time. Dave's band, the Colts, is playing Mum's favorite song, "Songbird" by Fleetwood Mac, which is all about love. Brains has joined them to sing, and his low and husky voice makes the lyrics sound really heartfelt.

Dave is waiting for Mum at the top of the room with his best men, Dan and Russ, beside him, and he looks so happy. His eyes are shining, and his grin stretches from ear to ear. His face is still a little flushed, but it doesn't matter. He still looks perfect in his morning suit.

Mum's eyes are glued to Dave's, as if they're the only two people in the whole room. Clover looks over at me and smiles. "We did good, Beanie," she whispers.

I nod back, too overcome to say anything.

♥ Chapter 22

After dinner in the beautiful wedding tent, I sit back in my chair and look around the room. Mills catches my eye and smiles and waves at me. Her table is just beside ours — she's sitting with Dad, Shelly, and Gracie, Finn, Polly, and Bailey. As Seth never replied to say he wasn't coming, there's an empty seat beside Polly where he should be sitting.

I'm at the head table with Mum and Dave, Clover, Monique, Russ, Dan, Gramps, Dave's parents, and Brains. Mum arranged a babysitter for Alex and Evie, and she took them back to Gramps's house straight after the ceremony. During the last song, Alex tried to strip his little suit off and run around naked. I knew his angel act was too good to last.

I'm really full after dinner. The food was amazing. Finn outdid himself and now he's taking a well-deserved rest, sitting beside Polly, chatting away to her and laughing a lot. I wonder if Mills is right? Maybe love really is in the air.

Clover nudges me. "Speeches, Beanie. Stop checking out Finn Hunter."

I laugh. "As if."

But she's right about the speeches being about to start. Russ stands up and taps his knife against his glass. "Pray silence for the bride. Sylvie would like to say a few words."

Everyone claps and cheers as Mum stands up. She looks around the tent for a long moment and then takes a deep breath. "Forgive me if I'm a little emotional," she begins. "It's been quite a day. Dave's not one for making speeches, so this is for both of us. First of all I have a few thank-yous. I want to start with Amy, Clover, and Monique, my beautiful bridesmaids. Amy and Clover also organized the entire wedding, and I'm really grateful to them and so proud of my little sister and my amazing daughter." Mum's eyes well up. I'm not far off crying myself. Clover takes my hand in hers and squeezes gently. I smile at her. "I'm incredibly proud of you both," Mum continues. "And I love you very much. Now I have some other people to thank. Firstly to Dan and Russ, Dave's best men . . ."

As Mum lists the rest of her thank-yous, I feel someone looking at me from the doorway of the tent, and I turn my head.

It's Seth. Clover's noticed him too.

"I told you he'd be here, Beanie," she says. "He still loves you, babes. I just know it."

Seth is staring straight at me. My heart starts to race, and I feel horribly nervous and sick. Could Clover be right? I raise my hand to wave and he waves back. I point at the empty seat at Mills's table and he nods. My head is so full of questions that I don't hear another word of Mum's speech, and Clover has to nudge me at the end so that I start clapping.

The applause rings out when Mum has finished, and Seth picks his way through the tables and sits down. He obviously didn't want to risk interrupting Mum by moving before. How sweet! He says something to Polly and then to Mills and Bailey. I catch Mills's eye and she smiles gently at me and gives a tiny nod in Seth's direction. "You OK?" she mouths at me.

I nod at her. But I'm not OK, not at all. Seth is *here*, at Mum's wedding. What does that mean? Is he here to hang out with Bailey? Has he taken pity on me and decided to show his face for a little while? Or could Clover possibly be right?

Next, Gramps says a few words about Sylvie, telling funny stories about the things she and Clover got up to when they were little. Then Clover proposes a toast. "To my beautiful sister on her wedding day. I wish you all the happiness in the world, Sylvie. You deserve it." Everyone *ahh*s.

And then Russ and Dan give a final toast to Mr. and Mrs. Marcus-Wildgust (they've decided to have a double-barreled name, even though it is rather long), and everyone clinks glasses.

"That's the speeches over," Clover says. "Now starts the fun bit — the dancing. Ready to shake a few tail feathers, Beanie?"

Brains and his band are already setting up on the wooden dance floor at the far end of the tent.

I nod. "Absolutely." But all I really want to do is talk to Seth.

Clover sees right through me. "Go and find him," she says. "I know you're dying to."

"I'm scared, Clover," I admit. "I miss him so much. I don't want to get upset on Mum's big day. Maybe he's just here to wish her good luck. He likes Mum."

Clover rolls her eyes. "He's not here for Sylvie. He's here to see *you*." She abruptly changes the subject. "Weren't they great speeches, Beanie? Sylvie's was lovely." Then adds casually, "Oh, hi, Seth. Didn't see you there."

He's here, standing so close I can almost reach out and touch him.

"Hi, Clover," he says.

"Nice to see you, Seth. I have to talk to Sylvie, I'm afraid, but I'll catch you later. Take care of my best friend, OK?"

"Amy," he says, after saying good-bye to Clover. His eyes are soft and gentle, just like the old Seth's.

"You came," I say.

"Yes. Can we talk?"

I nod silently. I follow Seth outside and we walk toward the front of Gramps's house. I point at the steps leading up to the front door. "Should we sit down?"

"Sure," he says. He sounds nervous. "Will your dress be OK?"

"It'll be fine." We sit beside each other, almost shoulder to shoulder. I stay quiet.

"You look beautiful," he says, breaking the silence.

"Thanks. You look nice too." He's wearing his

school trousers, a freshly ironed white shirt, and a light-blue tie that matches his eyes.

He laughs. "Mum told me I had to dress up. She's annoyed with me for being late, but I had to go into town first. I have something for you, a birthday present."

"You remembered?"

"Yes." He hands me a small package wrapped in white tissue paper. I open it carefully. Inside is a black box, the size of a matchbox. I open it. And inside that is a silver heart pendant on a delicate silver chain. I take it out.

"Turn it over," he says.

Engraved on the back is my name, the date of my birth, and then, underneath, the words, WITH LOVE ALWAYS, SETH.

I'm so overwhelmed I can barely breathe, and I have to suck air in, gasping loudly.

"Sorry, sorry," I murmur, putting my hands over my face in embarrassment.

"No, Amy, I'm the one who should be sorry. I was scared and I pushed you away. The truth is I miss you. I hate being without you. I thought coping with Polly's illness on my own would be easier, but I was wrong. I know I've hurt you and I have no right to expect anything, but can we start again?"

I lift my head and look at him. My mixed-up, annoying, gorgeous, kind boyfriend. And before I know what I'm doing I say, "Yes!"

Then I throw my arms around him and give him an almighty hug.

♥ Chapter 23

When Seth and I get back to the tent a little later—after talking for a while and, yes, kissing—loads of people are up and dancing to the Golden Lions's version of "Dancing Queen," including Mum and Clover, who are waving their arms in the air and singing along loudly. The sight makes me smile.

"There you are," Mills says when she sees us. She's holding Bailey's hand. "We've been looking everywhere for you two. Come and dance."

Monique has joined Mum and Clover now, and Russ is cheering her on. They wave over at me.

"Join us, Amy," Mum shouts over the music. "And Mills. All the girls."

"Sorry, Seth," I say to him. "Do you mind?"

"Not at all. I'll be right here, waiting for you. Have fun."

We head for the dance floor, and Mills whispers, "Is it back on? You and Seth, I mean?"

"Yes."

"Oh, Amy, that's brilliant," she squeals. "I'm so happy for you."

As soon as we reach the dance floor, the music starts to change. I realize what's happening only when Mum and Clover start belting out "Happy Birthday." Within seconds the whole tent has joined in. Then Finn walks toward me, holding a huge cake iced with pretty pink roses. It's blazing with fourteen sparkler candles. I'm so happy, I'm dancing inside.

Clover puts her arm around me. "Happy birthday, Beanie. Make a wish."

"I wish things could stay exactly as they are right this second forever and ever," I say.

"Me too, Beanie," she says. Her face is lit up by the candles and her eyes are sparkling, but they look sad too.

"What is it?"

"Later," she tells me. "We have cake to eat first, babes."

\* \* \*

I've stepped outside the tent to get some air. The Golden Lions are taking a break, and Seth is talking to Polly. I spot Clover sitting under one of Gramps's big old oak trees, her back leaning against the trunk. Brains is by her side.

"Hey, Amy," Brains says. "Keep my gal company, will ya? I have to ramp up the tunes in the tent again. You and Clover did the best job today. Nice work, babes."

"Thanks, Brains."

He gives me a kiss on the cheek. "You know how special you are to Clover, right? Never forget it." He walks off toward the tent, and I sit down carefully beside Clover, hoping the grass won't damage my dress.

"Don't worry about your dress," Clover says, reading my mind yet again. "It'll be fine. I do love a good wedding. And Sylvie and Dave look so happy." She sighs dreamily and rests her head on my shoulder. "Beanie, there's something I have to tell you. I can't put it off any longer."

"What is it?" I ask, feeling butterflies in my stomach.

"Brains asked me to marry him again."

"And?" I ask eagerly.

"I said yes." She shrugs. "Not right now, but sometime in the future. We belong together, me and Brains. Like Sylvie and Dave."

"Clover, that's amazing news!" I shriek. "Congratulations. Have you told Mum yet?"

"No, I wanted you to be the first to know."

I feel all warm and glowing inside. I grin at her. "Thanks."

She smiles back, then her face drops. "Beanie, there's something else. I don't really know how to say this. I've been offered an internship at *Vogue* in New York. Brains is going to be based there for a while with the band, recording their new album, so it's kind of perfect. I don't want to leave you, Beans. But . . . well . . . it's just such an amazing opportunity."

At that moment I finally understand what Mills meant by saying *If you love someone, you have to let them go.* I can't hold Clover back any more than I could force Seth to go out with me. Like Seth, Clover has to choose her own path, and she will come back to me when she's ready. And when she does, I'll be right here, waiting for her.

I take a deep breath and even though it hurts, I say, "New York! Of course you have to go, Clover. Are you crazy? Can I visit?"

"Abso-doodle-lutely, Beanie." She beams, her eyes twinkling.

And right then I realize how much this means to her and how worried she's been about letting me down. How could I stop her from going? Mills is right — Clover is destined for great things.

"That's part two of your birthday present, in fact," she adds. "A trip to the Big Apple in the summer, to stay with me. We'll have such fun, Beanie."

My heart almost leaps out of my chest. "Seriously? I can't wait. That will be brilliant."

"Are you sure you're OK with me going? Honest to Betsy?"

"Yes," I say, plastering my brightest smile on my face. "I'll miss you like crazy, Clover, you know I will. I love you to bits. But I'll be all right. I have Mills to talk to, and I'm back with Seth now. You were right, Clover, as always. Besides, there's always e-mail and Facebook and stuff."

She hugs me. "Coola boola. I'm so glad Seth finally came around. I knew he would. And I'll miss you too, Beanie. Every second of every day. I'll always be your number one fan, no matter what. And you have to keep writing — you have a gift. I've talked to Saffy, and if you're willing, she'd like you to babysit the problem pages while I'm in the U.S. of Amazing. What do you think? 'Amy Green, Teen Agony Queen.' Has a certain ring to it."

"On my ownio?"

"Yep, you're ready to fly solo, little bird. Up, up, and away. But you'll always be my best friend, Beanie. That will never change, I promise. Always and forever."

# ♥ Epilogue

Dear Amy,

I'm thirteen and I feel lonely and scared a lot of the time. I'm starting high school in September and I'm terrified. All my old friends are going to other schools and I'll be on my own. What if no one likes me? What if I end up eating lunch on my own every single day?

How do you make new friends if you're shy like me?

Can you help?

From Mollie in Dublin

\* \* \*

Dear Mollie,

    I know exactly how you feel, believe me. I was terrified of going into First Year too. But I have to say, it was a lot better than I ever imagined. And, yes, I think I can help you. . . .

## Acknowledgments

This is the last Amy Green book, and I must admit I'm very sad typing these final words of thanks. I've loved every minute of writing Amy and Clover's story and I'd like to first of all thank YOU, my dear reader, for sharing their journey with me.

Like organizing a wedding, writing and publishing a book is a team effort, and *Wedding Belles* would not have been possible without a lot of people's help. My name may be on the cover, but my second thank-you goes to my wonderful editor, Annalie Grainger, who has championed Amy's story from the very start. She knows the characters so well that she could easily write her own Amy Green adventure. Luckily Annalie and I are continuing our own adventures together, as she will also be editing my brand-new series.

My heartfelt thanks must also go to the amazing team at Walker: Gill, Maria, Jo, Sarah, Paul, Hannah, Jill, Molly, Sean, Hanna, Heidi, Katie, Sarah, Kate, Jan, and all the team. The wonderful Conor Hackett, Mr. Walker Books in Ireland and *Wedding Belles*'s best man, is also a joy to work with.

Thanks to my family: Mum, Dad, Kate, Emma, and Richard; and to my own crew — Ben, Sam, Amy, and Jago. Plus my dear friends Tanya, Nicky, and Andrew.

I have a wonderful support network of writing and book friends in Ireland, and I'd like to especially thank Martina Devlin, Judi Curtin, Marita Conlon-McKenna, Tom Donegan, Kim Harte, Grainne Clear, Claire Hennessy, Vanessa O'Loughlin, Oisín McGann, David Maybury, and Jenny and Aoife in CBI for their friendship and help.

Philippa Milnes-Smith and Peta Nightingale are the kind of agents you dream about—smart, kind, funny, and great at their jobs. I'm blessed to have them on my team.

I must mention my original teen editor and fount of all knowledge, Kate Gordon. Kate has been part of Team Amy right from the start. She's now heading toward college—clever girl—but I know she will always be an Amy Greenster at heart.

This book is also dedicated to my Young Editors: Alice Mountstephens, Niamh Brennan, Iseult Murphy, Ellen Byrne, and Sophie Schouwenburg. They all did a brilliant job on this book. And I promised that I would say hi to Emma Quigley because she asked me so nicely.

As an ex-children's bookseller, I know how important (and cool) booksellers are. Thanks to everyone who has been so good to me over the last six years: David O'Callaghan at Eason, the fantastic Dubray gang, and the gangs at the Gutter Bookshop, Raven Books, and Bridge Street Books.

And finally to the unsung heroes of the book world, the librarians. I have the great pleasure of working with the lovely Marian Keyes on a regular basis, and I can tell you, the libraries of Dun Laoghaire/Rathdown are in good hands.

Thank you, all of you, for making my writing and book life so full of joy.

Readers, please do drop me a line. I love hearing from Amy Greensters. My e-mail is sarah@askamygreen.com. Or check out the Ask Amy Green fan page on Facebook.

Best always,
Sarah XXX